Live Laugh Love

Copyright © Jennie Alexander 2016. All rights reserved.
The moral right of Jennie Alexander to be identified as author of this work has been asserted in accordance with the Copyright, Designs and Patents Act 1988.

No part of this publication may be reproduced, stored in a retrieval system or transmitted in any form or by any means, without the prior permission in writing of the publisher, nor to be otherwise circulated in any form of binding or cover other than that in which it is published without a similar condition, including this condition, being imposed on the subsequent purchaser.
This novel is a work of fiction. Names, characters and incidents are the product of the author's imagination. Any resemblance to actual persons, living or dead, is purely coincidental.

Live Laugh Love

Jennie Alexander

Also by Jennie Alexander

The Beach Hut
Winnifred Cottage
The Reunion Party
A Nice Glass of Red
The Writer

THE COCO CLUB SERIES
Genevieve
Blue-Belle
Delphine
Lily

CHRISTMAS NOVELLAS
Tied with a Ribbon
Home for Christmas

For more information:

www.JennieAlexander.co.uk

JennieAlexander@hotmail.co.uk

*The greatest happiness of life is the conviction
that we are loved — loved for ourselves, or rather,
loved in spite of ourselves."*

— Victor Hugo

PROLOGUE

Hope tapped on the back door and without waiting for an answer let herself into Josie's house.

'Hello, it's only me.' She went through into the kitchen where Josie was sitting at the island in the middle of the kitchen huddled over her computer. She glanced over her shoulder.

'Hi, coffee's on the table. I won't be a sec.'

'What are you buying now?' asked Hope, peering at the screen.

'Nothing actually. Sadly. I'm trying to sell something.'

Hope sat down and was about to ask what she was selling but sipped her coffee instead, knowing she wouldn't get a proper answer until she had her scatty friend's full attention.

After a few seconds of squealing insults at the screen, Josie came to sit at the table, still frowning with the exertion of it all.

Hope's raised eyebrows asked the obvious question.

'I'm trying to sell a holiday.' Josie sighed dramatically. 'Yeah, I won a holiday in a competition – a walking holiday of all things! In the relaxing hills of Derbyshire. Can you imagine? Me? In the relaxing hills of Derbyshire? Honestly!'

'Sounds wonderful. But no, I can't imagine it.' Hope smiled and sipped. She couldn't imagine Josie walking anywhere for pleasure, let alone relaxing. 'But why did you enter the competition if you didn't want the prize?'

'I didn't expect to win! Well, not the first prize. I didn't want that. I was after the third prize – a rowing machine. It's Ross's birthday next month, and I saw it and thought he'd love it.'

'You could just buy one?' suggested Hope, trying, not very hard, to hide her amusement.

'Mm, yes, I suppose,' said Josie vaguely, as if she hadn't really thought of that. 'But anyway, this was more fun. Apart from the holiday I've now got to get rid of.'

'Crikey, what I'd do for a holiday.'

'Do you want it? Please, Hope, take it.'

'No, I can't. But thanks anyway.'

'Why can't you?'

'I can't just take off and leave everything. The business won't run itself.'

Josie was checking the computer screen to see if anyone had bid on the holiday yet and at the same time pulled a load of washing from the machine into a basket at her feet.

'But it's your kind of holiday, isn't it?'

'Sort of.'

Josie abandoned the washing and sat back down. She had a thoughtful look on her face. 'OK, so imagine you could go anywhere in the world for a holiday. Where would you go?'

'Oh, that's easy.' Hope didn't have her handbag with her, but she pictured the magazine article she'd torn out a couple of years ago and kept inside. 'I'd go to The Harmony Wellbeing Retreat in Indonesia – Bali.'

Josie grimaced. It wasn't her kind of holiday at all, but she could tell just by the look on her friend's face, the way it instantly lit up, that the thought of it alone was doing her good. Hope gazed into her coffee. Cradling the mug gently in her hands, she stared straight ahead, a faraway look on her face as if merely the mention of Bali had transported her the 7,000 miles across the globe to Indonesia.

'It's my absolute dream holiday. Sunshine; a beautiful paradise island; the welcome of its people, their spirit and culture.' Hope regained focus, looking almost surprised to see herself in Josie's kitchen. She sighed. 'I've wanted to go for years, but…'

'But what? Why don't you just go?'

Hope gave a little shrug.

'Well, it's not money, is it? You must be loaded!'

Hope looked a little shocked at first and then smiled as Josie gave her a cheeky wink. She was out of her chair again, fussing with the washing basket.

'How many books have you got out there now?'

Hope had been writing cookery books for children for almost fifteen years. Her 'Cook with Hope' series had become a huge success, each book selling even better than the last.

'I've just completed my tenth book. It'll be published next month, November, in time for Christmas.'

'A perfect time to take a break then, eh? And what about all your other cooky stuff? That's doing well isn't it?'

'Other cooky stuff' was Hope's own range of specially designed cookery equipment for children, to accompany her books. She'd also opened a shop three years ago and ran it together with Martha, her friend and business partner. Demand was increasing so fast, they were in the process of setting up a mail order website.

'Yes, it's doing great. Brilliant actually.'

Josie came back to the table, plonked herself down, and looked Hope directly in the eye.

'So, what's stopping you? You may be the main bread-winner, but you need a break too.'

'What do you mean?' Hope was unsure of what Josie was implying.

'Well, Laurie has a good life, doesn't he? You've been keeping him in a lifestyle that he's become very accustomed to.' Josie pulled a face to show she wasn't being overly serious. 'I just think you deserve a holiday that's all.'

'Laurie's great,' said Hope. 'He's always been very supportive of me. We both decided it wasn't necessary for him to get another job after his redundancy, and this way he can concentrate on his art. He does sell things, you know, occasionally. And for good money too.'

'I know. I'm not getting at your lovely Laurie. You two have it all working out great. It's just that you don't really do much just for yourself, out of work I mean.

And this sounds like something you really want to do. Would Laurie go with you?'

'No, no, it's not his sort of thing at all. He thinks my collection of relaxation CDs is amusing. What's amusing is that I never have time to relax and listen to them!'

'Exactly!'

There was silence as Hope actually thought about it seriously for a moment. She looked intently at Josie, her mind racing. Could this really be possible?

'What about my mother? I check in on her two or three times a week, at least.'

Josie held up her hand and stopped Hope in her tracks. 'We can all take turns; Laurie, me, and Martha – she'd love to help. And before you say it; Sara will be fine. She's happily settled at uni – she won't miss you!'

Hope grimaced. Josie had certainly hit that nail squarely on the head; Sara, her twenty-two-year-old daughter, would be delighted to have her mother disappear to the other side of the world for a few weeks, leaving her with her father all to herself.

It would take a lot of planning, maybe a good six months. She counted ahead - Bali would be perfect in April, just at the beginning of the dry season. Maybe it *was* possible.

Chapter 1

Six months later

Hope stood in the guest bedroom looking at the jumble of items sprawled across the bed. She plonked herself down trying to figure out how everything was going to fit into her suitcase.

A very expensive bottle of suntan lotion rolled towards her, and she popped the lid off, breathing in the scent, and was immediately transported to a tropical paradise with turquoise skies, shimmering sunshine and warm soft-as-a-feather breezes.

Her packing was almost finished but she would have to be ruthless with these last few things – or very inventive. This time tomorrow she would be on her way to Heathrow Airport, and from there an eighteen-hour flight to Bali, changing at Hong Kong. She could hardly believe this day had finally arrived.

The phone rang and Hope snatched it up from the bedside table, hoping it was Laurie – she was expecting him home ages ago.

'Hello?'

'Hi, it's me, Josie. I'm just tidying my attic and guess what I've found?'

For just a moment, Hope wondered what on earth had prompted Josie to tidy her attic on a freezing cold Thursday afternoon in April. But she decided not to pursue it.

'I don't know. What have you found?'

'A bible!'

Silence.

'I found a bible. You can take it with you, you'll need one.'

'Josie, why would I need a bible?'

'Well, you know, you'll be doing all that praying and hallelujah-ing and things. This will be perfect bedtime reading. You are allowed books, aren't you?'

Hope grinned. 'Yes, of course I'm allowed books. I'm going to a luxury wellbeing retreat Josie; this is a huge treat for me, it's not a punishment. The idea is to relax, have time to myself to think and clear my head. I'm planning to take some yoga classes and meditation, but I don't think I'll actually be doing any praying. But thank-you anyway. It was very sweet of you to think of me.'

'Right OK. But I'll bring it over anyway, just in case. And I'll get back in the attic, see what else I can find. There're stacks of books up there. They've been there since we moved in, I'd forgotten all about them. OK, I'll catch you later.'

Hope hung up the phone, shaking her head like a stunned cartoon character. She smiled at the thought of her whirlwind friend, such a good friend, rummaging in her attic looking for books for her. She didn't have the heart to tell her she'd already packed her e-book reader which could hold thousands of books. But anyway, it would be no use protesting; once Josie had an idea in mind, there was no stopping her.

Hope heard a noise from downstairs and stepped out onto the landing. She peered over the stair rail to the hall below.

'Laurie? Is that you?'

There was no response and she returned to her packing. It was probably Lulu the cat, jumping up at the front door handle, trying to get in. Well, she could wait, as punishment for tiddling on the rug. She was still only a kitten, but she would have to learn.

Hope had bought some new hand luggage for the journey. It was expensive, a real extravagance. She pulled the leather holdall across the bed and peered inside, checking the contents yet again. There was a variety of magazines and of course her Kindle; a selection of toiletries to keep her comfortable and fresh throughout the incredibly long flight, already placed in a clear, plastic bag; a soft cashmere shawl in case she got chilly on the plane and could hopefully snuggle down for a snooze, and also a book on Bali.

She zipped the holdall closed, and smoothed her hand over the quality leather, marvelling at how fortunate she was to be finally heading off on her dream holiday. She closed her eyes, butterflies of excitement dancing in her stomach as she tried to imagine herself in just a couple of days' time, sitting cross-legged, meditating peacefully, in a large, silent hall full of other cross-legged meditators.

This was something Hope was particularly looking forward to - the peace and quiet. No phone calls, texts or emails. Just solitude and silence. Although, she had to admit it was a little daunting too. This was the first time in years she would have so much time to herself without some distraction or other. There would be no business commitments or family needs pulling her in all directions. She would be alone for six whole weeks. She felt like an excited child going to the seaside, and just couldn't wait to get there.

Hope squeezed a few more things into her case including a leather journal she'd bought. She thought she might be inspired to write about her experiences while she was in Bali, or maybe even start a novel – something completely different from writing about cookery for children anyway.

She and Laurie had often joked about producing travel guides together. They would travel the world one day; she would do the writing and he would draw comical cartoon illustrations. One day.

Hope sighed, tucking the journal deeper into her case for protection and feeling a sudden pang of guilt over her solo trip.

Laurie had gone out earlier in the afternoon to his art supplies place and then on to somewhere else, but she couldn't remember exactly what he'd said. He'd been rather vague, she remembered that much, and of course she'd been totally preoccupied at the time. She frowned now, feeling guilty again, for not paying better attention.

She checked the time, working out when to prepare dinner as they had planned to share a special meal tonight. Deciding to take a break for a cup of tea, she went downstairs and switched the kettle on before checking her mobile phone which she'd left on the worktop. She hoped there would be a missed call or message from Laurie but there was neither. She rang his mobile but after a few rings it went to voicemail, and so she left a quick message.

Suddenly feeling very anxious and not knowing what else to do, Hope opened the front door and peered out beyond the long drive, over the tall boundary hedges, hoping to catch a glimpse of Laurie's car, willing it to turn into their road returning home.

She caught sight of her worried expression in the huge mirror hanging in the hall, and from habit, unclipped her long dark hair, tidying the wispy strands behind her ears before clipping it up again.

It was quickly sinking in that this really wasn't like Laurie at all. He was supposed to be home by now and it wasn't like him not to call and let her know where he was, why he was late and when he'd be back. That's just the way they were with each other.

She closed the door just as Lulu the kitten skittered past her, straight for the kitchen and her food bowl. It still surprised her – the way Laurie suddenly let her have a cat – he'd always hated them. And then out of the blue, when she couldn't think of anything she wanted for her birthday a few weeks ago, he'd said he knew of someone whose cat had just had kittens. And did she want one?

He'd always joked that cats were for lonely old ladies, but she was only forty-three. She was sure there was no significance to this change of heart.

She smiled at Lulu who in her eagerness to get to her food had actually put one of her front paws in the bowl.

Hope stared out the kitchen window, hands wrapped around her mug of tea. It had been a long hard winter and the crocuses were just peeking through the grass under the slowly awakening Laburnum tree. They would be in full bloom and maybe even finished by the time she got back. It was difficult to imagine being away from everything for so long. She'd got a little tearful yesterday when saying good-bye to her mother; they'd never been apart for so long. But on the upside, her mother would enjoy the company of everyone popping in to see her.

As she sipped her tea, she shuffled through some papers on the table. There were lists for everything; a list for Laurie for while she was away, a list of things to talk to Laurie about before she went, and several of her own never-ending To-Do lists.

She left the mess of papers where it was, unable to concentrate. Still clutching her mug, she paced the kitchen wondering if this was how Josie felt all the time.

Josie was the epitome of someone with ants in their pants, always anxious, never able to sit still for a second.

After several circuits around the kitchen table, she threw the dregs of tea in the sink and rinsed the mug. Back at the table she picked up her list for this week, feeling great satisfaction at the long line of ticks running down the page, marking the completion of almost every task.

She had dealt with all the household accounts so Laurie wouldn't have to worry about what bills might need paying, it was all taken care of. She had stocked the freezer with his favourite foods, and even made some individual sized portions of fish pie and lasagne so all he had to do was pop them in the oven.

And as a final attempt to appease her guilt for abandoning him for six weeks, she had gone on a Christmas-style shopping spree filling the cupboards with all sorts of treats for her wonderful husband. She'd bought him the disgusting-smelling crab pâté he loved. She was quite happy for him to gorge himself on that while she was away. And the biggest box she could find of his favourite chocolates - he was slightly embarrassed at his passion for champagne truffles. Hope smiled at the thought of him in his armchair at the end of the day secretly scoffing the lot.

Laurie was a man's man in every other way; he enjoyed a pint with his friends at the local pub, followed rugby and Formula One. She gave a little sigh - she'd miss him over the next few weeks. Over in the corner by the wine rack she spotted the ridiculously expensive bottle of brandy she'd bought him – particularly pleased now that she had. This was one very special thing that was usually reserved just for Christmas.

Anyway, Hope needn't have felt guilty for going away. Laurie had been absolutely fine about it. She'd expected a small kick-back from him which would have been fair enough. After all, they hadn't taken a holiday together for years and here she was going off on her own.

When she'd first mentioned it, he'd been a little surprised but then immediately warmed to the idea, said that she deserved a break. He'd been nothing but supportive and encouraging and assured her that he could look after himself. Bless him for that.

Hope picked up her list for today. She had ticked off most of the items except for 'Packing' and 'Phone Sara'. Laurie had told her that Sara said she would phone before her mother left for Bali – a lot of messages from Sara came through Laurie lately. But if Sara was going to phone, she was cutting it a bit fine.

They spoke infrequently. Even at twenty-two, Sara hadn't outgrown the typical teenage attitude that reacted to every innocent enquiry from her mother as though it were an interrogation. And more recently Hope found it difficult to talk to her daughter, knowing what she did.

Everyone thought Sara was at university in Leicester, well into her third year of studying Business and Accounting. But Hope knew that, in fact, she had dropped her studies just over a year ago. She also knew she was no longer living in the house she'd shared with three other students even though she still collected her post from there, having recently thanked her mother for her birthday card and the generous cheque she'd slipped inside. But as to the reason for all the secrecy, Hope knew nothing at all.

But what could she do? Her daughter was no longer a child, free to do whatever she wanted without obligation to tell anyone anything. Although there was the matter of the monthly allowance cheques Sara was still cashing. Hope winced at the deception and stopped herself from thinking about it.

For a mad moment she'd wondered if Laurie knew what was going on. He and Sara had always been especially close. It was on the tip of her tongue to ask as she was writing Sara's birthday card, but she lost her nerve, maybe she didn't want to know. She couldn't make up her mind how to handle things or what to do for the best. This was definitely something she would dedicate some thinking time to when she got to Bali, that and a few other things.

Hope pulled out a chair and sat down. On a clean sheet of paper, she wrote a title 'Things to Think About' at the top and underneath wrote her daughter's name in capital letters. She jotted down a few other things that immediately came to mind. 'Bigger Premises' – they'd already outgrown the cookery shop and it was beginning to look cluttered and disorganised. 'More Staff' - they definitely needed an extra pair of hands whether they moved or not. It was difficult with just her and Martha having to cover for each other. Martha had taken a lot of time off lately and Hope had had to spend more time in the shop – time when she could have been writing. She ended the list with 'Cookery Books Abroad' and 'Cook Kits' - a couple of business ideas that had been floating around in her head for some time.

She pushed the list to the side of the table ready to be packed. A dish of lasagne sat on the draining board ready to go into the oven – one of their favourite meals. It was to be her 'last supper' she joked, their last chance for a good chat together but she reflected now that Laurie hadn't seemed that keen. Tomorrow afternoon, she would be busy with last minute preparations and getting ready to leave for the airport.

Hope glanced at the clock; it was six o'clock. She wondered whether she should put the lasagne in the oven now. Laurie would probably be home any minute, all smiling and apologetic. She sighed, muttering, 'Come on Laurie, where the hell are you?'

Despite expecting and willing the phone to ring, she still jumped when it did and snatched it from the wall.

'Hello?'

'Hi, it's me.' Laurie didn't sound smiley or apologetic.

'Laurie, for goodness' sake, where are you? I was getting worried. Is everything alright? Are you OK?'

'Calm down Hope, everything's fine. I'm fine. Listen…'

'I phoned you and I left a message. Why didn't you phone me back?' She stopped, unnerved by Laurie's tone. Something wasn't right. 'I've got a lasagne here;

we're supposed to be having dinner and everything.' And now even her own voice sounded strange to her. A couple of seconds of silence followed before Laurie spoke.

'Hope just leave the lasagne. I want you to come to The Yorkshire Grey pub. You know where it is, on the Woollenwick Road?'

'Well, yes, I know where it is, but…'

'Just get in the car and make your way there. I'll be with you shortly.'

Hope's mind was racing. What was going on? Something to do with her holiday? Was he planning a surprise evening out? Perhaps Sara had come down. But he knew she didn't really like having things sprung on her. And anyway, there was something about his tone of voice. She forced a smile, tried to keep her own voice light.

'Laurie. What's this all about? Just come home, can't you?'

'No, I can't. Hope we need to talk. I have something to tell you. I'm leaving shortly and I'll be at The Yorkshire Grey in about fifteen minutes. I'll see you there.'

'Where are you now?' But it was too late, he'd already rung off.

Slowly she hung up the phone, and gazed around the kitchen, momentarily immobilized, trying to take in and fathom out all the possible implications of that very brief and odd conversation.

Mechanically, she picked up her car keys and lifted her handbag from the back of a chair. Despite the urgency in Laurie's voice or maybe because of it, she felt a reluctance to rush. Slowly and calmly, she put on her coat, got into her car and drove off.

Chapter 2

Josie Bell had promised her husband she would go up into the attic to dig out his old record albums. They were mostly from the eighties, his teenage years, and he'd asked after them just last week.

Ross had reminded her again this afternoon. As he was heading out the door on his way to the Butlers Golf Club AGM, he prompted her to retrieve his records, thinking he was being helpful in giving her something to do while he was out. She'd smiled wryly at that.

And so, she'd dutifully gone up into the attic and began sorting through the dusty piles of albums but had soon got distracted when she found the old bible and then all the other books.

Josie glanced through the records; The Human League, Spandau Ballet, Blondie and loads of other names she'd sort of heard of but that weren't from her youth. At almost fifty, Ross was twenty years older than her. One of his friends had recently given a seventies themed party - everyone seemed to be doing it lately and now Ross was planning for them to throw an eighties one – except, of course, he wanted it to be bigger and better than all the others. Josie just thought it would be rather nice to go to a party where they played music from the current century for a change.

It took her ages to pull out all the records she thought he'd want and haul them across the attic, stacking them up carefully next to the pile of paperbacks she'd chosen for Hope with the Bible balanced carefully on top.

It was getting cold up there now and Josie decided she'd had enough for the day. Standing up straight with a stiff back and brushing dust from her hands, she glanced out the little round window down into the dusky street below. She saw Hope pulling off her drive and wondered where she was going, noting at the same time that Laurie's car wasn't there. Surely, she would be finishing her packing ready for her holiday. And then Josie smiled, knowing her friend, she probably had absolutely everything completely organised by now. How she envied Hope's sense of calm organisation; everything always under control as well as being a wife and mother, and a successful businesswoman too. Josie sighed, reassuring herself that there was still plenty of time for all that.

This time tomorrow her friend would be off to Bali for six whole weeks – Josie would miss her terribly. When Hope had first mentioned her dream of going on a spiritual retreat, Josie couldn't see the appeal of that type of holiday. She'd much rather go back to Spain or hopefully Florida one day. But just these last few weeks, things were getting on top of her, and she was beginning to see the appeal of escaping for a little while.

Having lugged everything down from the attic and having nearly fell off the ladder at least three times, she sat on the bottom rung, catching her breath. In a minute, she would pile everything up in one of the spare rooms.

The huge attic in the steep pitched roof was a fantastic space and she'd earmarked it as her own since their very first viewing of the house over three years ago, just before they were married. She imagined it fitted out as a work area - perhaps she'd take up some hobbies or maybe even start her own business but as yet it was still just a junk room. Hope, with her cookery business, was her inspiration and Josie wondered if she could ever be as successful at something.

Ross was great, he didn't mind her not going out to work, he even said he liked her being at home and Josie knew she had such a lot to be grateful for - after all he had rescued her from a lifetime of working in Tesco.

Life had changed in almost unbelievable ways since she'd met Ross. She was the second eldest of seven children and their tiny, terraced house was very crowded. Although she loved all her brothers and sisters, aside from their company, there was never much of anything in the way of treats or luxuries, not even on special occasions.

Her mum worked early mornings cleaning in an office block. Her dad left when she was ten although she didn't remember the event making any significant impact on anything particular. He came back occasionally and for a while he and their mum were happy. But it never lasted; soon enough they would argue about money. He never stayed for more than a few days at a time to the point where neither Josie nor her siblings paid any attention to his comings and goings.

Her mum described herself as the Bingo Queen and the local community centre was always the most likely place to find her, not that they ever needed to.

Josie remembered when she was sixteen and the thrill of getting a part-time job at the nearby Tesco superstore. At first, she worked only on Saturdays, but her speed and accuracy meant she was soon offered extra hours in the evenings. Although the Bingo Queen threatened them all with unspeakable punishment if they didn't attend school, fortunately there was never much emphasis on the production of homework and so Josie was able to work Thursday and Friday evenings too.

The money she earned at the time seemed like a fortune to her and for the first time ever she was able to buy a few fashionable clothes, a little make-up and most weeks a few sweets for the young ones to share.

Her mum never asked her for any of her earnings although on occasions she would ask to borrow a few pounds. Josie never got it back, but she didn't mind. A friend of hers at school had a Saturday job in a shoe shop and she had to give her parents half of what she earned. At the time, Josie thought she was very lucky.

One day in her lunch hour she wandered through the local market heading straight for the little jewellery stall she liked. She was thinking of having some extra piercings in her ear and bought some tiny studs in readiness. And then she saw a necklace, the sort that has a name suspended in the middle between the chain on either side. This one was silver and in the middle the words 'Bingo Queen'. She just had to get it. She gave it to her mum after work on Saturday just as her mum was getting ready to go out. She unfolded the little paper bag and took out the necklace, holding it gently in her hands, just staring at it for what seemed like a very long time. Josie thought she was going to cry but instead her mum pulled her into a tight hug.

'Thank-you sweetheart. It's the best thing. I'll wear it forever.'

And she did.

Josie pushed the folding ladder back up into the attic and closed the door. She stood on the landing aware of the soft deep pile carpet beneath her feet, as she looked across at the span of the house and the many doors leading off the landing into bedrooms and bathrooms, more than they would ever need.

If her mum could see her now - in this gorgeous house in this picturesque village, she would say something to the effect of 'how well she had done for herself'.

Josie's mum died at the age of forty-five when Josie herself was only twenty. It was left to her and her older sister to look after the rest of the family. With Josie working full-time at Tesco, she was now the main earner.

By her mid-twenties, she'd been at the supermarket for almost ten years and had given up any hope of doing anything better. Her dreams had never been huge; she had liked the idea of working as a receptionist perhaps in a big hotel or a smart office, but there was never the time or spare finances to attend a college course.

Josie remembered the first time she'd seen Ross come into the shop when she was working one evening. He looked incredibly smart and a little out of place but in a good way – he stood out. He was wearing a grey suit, crisp white shirt and a lilac tie, and was carrying a bottle of wine. She watched him appear at the front of the checkouts and then he spotted her at the end watching him. He gave her a cheeky wink and made an immediate beeline for her.

He said the rather clichéd silly things like, 'What's a pretty girl like you doing working here on a Friday night?' but Josie laughed anyway. He was just teasing, she knew that, but it was nice to have a customer who had a sense of humour and time to chat, rather than the most of them who dashed through her checkout, just about managing a 'thank-you' before they hurried on to their evening.

For extra money, she still worked the late evenings on Thursday and Friday. Her routine was always the same - she worked until nine o'clock and then got off home as quick as she could, cooked herself something to eat, ate in front of the television and then went to bed.

Occasionally she would go out with friends but mostly whenever overtime was offered, she would take that instead; her family relied on her earnings.

A couple of weeks later Ross came to her checkout again. And then again, the following week, and the week after that. They chatted a little more each time. On one occasion, he stood behind a woman with a huge amount of shopping, her trolley almost overflowing. A member of staff offered him a faster checkout further down the shop. Josie looked up to see Ross politely refuse, saying he would rather wait in this queue. She could feel her face redden and was all fingers and thumbs as she attempted to scan the customer's shopping at breakneck speed.

'Hello gorgeous, how are you on this beautiful summer's evening?'

'I'm fine, thanks.' She didn't know what else to say to him. She knew she wasn't gorgeous as such, but she thought her grey-green eyes were quite attractive and her long blonde hair was often the envy of her friends. She wished she were taller than her petite five foot three, but at least high heels could put that right.

'Do you never get a Friday off?'

'No, it doesn't really work like that. I would have to take it as holiday.'

'What time do you finish?'

'Nine o'clock.' Josie was sure this very smart businessman couldn't possibly be chatting her up. He was probably only making polite conversation with her, the way he most likely did with every checkout girl, but the way he was looking at her and smiling at her was making her stomach somersault. And anyway, she was just enjoying it.

'And are you going out somewhere afterwards? With friends? Boyfriend?'

'Oh no, I'm not going anywhere. Just home.' She was about to tell him about her large family that she was partly responsible for looking after, but something stopped her. 'And actually, I don't have a boyfriend.'

Ross threw his few items of shopping into a carrier bag, taking out his wallet to pay and flashing her the biggest smile. 'So, how about I meet you outside just after nine and I take you for a drink and a bite to eat? How does that sound?'

Josie smiled back, nodding in agreement. 'OK'.

They went to a pub in the middle of the shopping centre, it had been newly refurbished with lots of chrome and black leather seating. Out with her friends, Josie would have ordered a half pint of lager for herself but remembering that Ross always bought a bottle of wine, she asked for a glass of red instead. The barman asked her whether she would like the Merlot, Malbec or apparently, the Pinot Noir was very good. She didn't have a clue and looked to Ross for help. He recommended the Merlot, ordered two glasses, and took her to sit in a secluded corner. She'd never been on a date with a man who drank wine before, let alone one who knew all the different types. Apart from that one moment of uncomfortableness, she felt totally at ease with Ross.

After he dropped her off at home in his almost new Range Rover, Josie closed the front door, leaning back against it, relishing the rare silence of the house. It was late and everyone was in bed. As much as she loved her family; all her brothers and sisters, she offered a silent prayer that hopefully tonight, just maybe, her luck in life had changed.

From then on, she and Ross went out every single Friday night and often in the week too. He seemed happy to listen to her constant chatting about her family or work, only zoning out on occasions, and then swiftly bringing the conversation back to his business in property management or golf.

He took her to some fancy restaurants where he knew the owners and everyone who worked there. She liked that he was popular and had so many friends. He would always insist on paying for her, saying she couldn't possibly afford to pay, on her pittance of a shop girl's wages. Sometimes he said things like that, but she knew he didn't mean to hurt her feelings. Her pittance was, after all, helping to feed a family of seven.

A long weekend holiday to Ibiza was where he produced a diamond ring and asked her to marry him.

Even though he was twenty years older than her, he didn't look anywhere near his age, and she had no qualms in saying yes immediately. He was different to the young men of her age. It seemed her experiences in life had matured her way beyond her years and Ross was much more of a match for her.

She was a little concerned at some of his rather old-fashioned ideas about marriage although his insistence that she give up working in Tesco immediately and concentrate on house-hunting was one idea she didn't disagree with.

They had been married for three years now and true to his word, Ross had looked after her. And although she never wanted to hear the beep of a grocery scanner again, she was restless for something; hopefully something more challenging than being a checkout girl. She felt the need to be able to contribute financially too - the problem was she didn't even have a clue as to what else she could do. And unfortunately, Ross wasn't exactly encouraging in this area.

Chapter 3

Hope drove into the car park of The Yorkshire Grey Pub, her troubled mind unable to focus. On autopilot, she remembered nothing of the journey but looking at the digital clock on the dashboard, she noted that it had taken her exactly thirteen minutes to get there. Was that an omen?

She had come to the conclusion that this wasn't a surprise going away meal or anything like that. Laurie's tone of voice had been very odd, she couldn't identify exactly what it was. It had been calm but uneasy. It was probably something to do with Sara – perhaps Laurie had found out about her leaving university. But why did they have to come all the way out here to talk about it? Hope took a deep breath, long and slow, trying to relax the anxious tangle of her insides.

The car park was busy but after a quick scan around, she could see that Laurie's car wasn't there. She drove on and parked in the furthest corner, suddenly and inexplicably, feeling the need to have the edge - to be able to see without being seen. She sat there with the engine and lights turned off, staring at the entrance to the car park, watching as cars drove in waiting anxiously to see Laurie's car arrive.

Her mind wandered as she gazed past the car park to the fields beyond. She loved living here in this Surrey village with its beautiful countryside and still only a hop away from London.

After a while, for what felt like the hundredth time that day, Hope found herself wondering where her husband was. And yet again, the combination of cursing him while aware that perhaps she should be worrying about him made her feel guilty.

'Come on Laurie. For god's sake!' she muttered.

After another fifteen minutes, she no longer felt guilty. What was this game he was playing? Getting her all the way out here and then not turning up? She pulled her mobile phone from her handbag knowing it was inconceivable, sitting here in this silence, that she could have missed a text message or a call. She rang his phone, no answer. And then she rang the home phone just because, really, she didn't know what else to do.

She slammed her phone onto the passenger seat, glaring at it, willing it to ring back.

'He'll be here any minute,' she muttered, trying to calm herself. She thought ahead twenty-four hours to when she'd be on her way to a relaxing retreat and the guilt rose to the surface again. She'd be leaving Laurie alone for six weeks - she really shouldn't be cross with him for keeping her waiting a few minutes.

She allowed herself a little smile; this time tomorrow she would be at Heathrow Airport, in the executive lounge, maybe sipping a gin and tonic.

And that thought made her realise that right now she was ready for a glass of wine and it suddenly occurred to her how silly she was being, staying in her car, hiding out of the way. She was perfectly capable of walking into a pub and ordering a drink for herself. After all, she was Hope Clements – successful writer and businesswoman.

With a glass of red wine and herself tucked in a cosy corner with full vantage of the door, she berated herself for her silliness. True, she was the only woman in the pub on her own, but it was no big deal she told herself. And anyway, Laurie would be here any second.

Hope twiddled the stem of her glass between finger and thumb and tried not to look like someone who was waiting for someone. It was quiet in the pub, and she wished it was busier. She looked at her watch yet again and frowned, then sighed and looked up at the door as two young women came inside.

Just for something to do, she took out her phone and began deleting old messages. A while later when her glass was almost empty, she rang Laurie again. It rang four times then switched to voicemail. She hung up. Redialled, hung up. Redialled, hung up. Redialled. Over and over like a jilted lovesick teenager.

Hope stared into the last of her drink, deciding it wouldn't be wise to get another. She decided to finish her wine and then leave. As a compromise, she would make these last few sips last another ten minutes, but that's all.

Fifteen minutes later, just after eight o'clock, Hope left The Yorkshire Grey Pub and drove home.

She slammed the front door with such force Lulu the kitten, who'd come into the hall to greet her, shot off into the living room to hide behind an armchair. Hope, annoyed with herself for frightening the cat, threw her coat on the settee and called out soothing noises.

'Come here you stupid cat!' But she couldn't keep the anger from her voice and Lulu scampered into the corner of the room behind the desk. 'Oh, you can just stay there then.'

She stomped into the kitchen and flicked on the light and then took a glass from the cupboard, banging it down on the worktop. The wine rack was fully stocked with Laurie's favourites, all rather expensive. She'd chosen them carefully but took one now and unceremoniously yanked off the screw top. And then she stopped and closed her eyes as if in prayer.

'Where are you Laurie? Please, just come home.'

She replaced the lid on the wine bottle, leaving the glass empty. Lulu came into the kitchen and squeezed her soft, fluffy fur against Hope's ankles, weaving timidly in and out. She scooped her up into her arms. 'Where is he eh? Should I start worrying? I know, there's probably some silly explanation for all this.'

Hope heard footsteps outside a second before the doorbell rang. She dashed to the hall and stopped dead. Through the frosted glass, she could make it out easily;

two people dressed in dark clothing, wearing fluorescent jackets, and hats – official hats. There was the squawk and crackle of a walkie-talkie.

As she reached forward to open the door, she knew without doubt, this was the time to start worrying.

Chapter 4

'Mrs Clements?' The young policeman spoke first.
'Yes. It's Laurie, isn't it? What's happened?'
'Can we come in please, Mrs Clements?' This time it was the policewoman who spoke. She was also very young, and Hope couldn't reconcile what she knew was to be terrible news with the fact that it was going to be these two very young people who were going to give it to her.

'Please, just tell me.'

The policewoman continued. 'Mrs Clements, please let us come inside and we can talk properly.' She stepped inside the hallway and was regarding Hope carefully, leaving her colleague to close the front door.

'Just tell me, please, for god's sake.'

'OK, there's been an accident. Your husband's car came off the road and hit a tree. It landed in a ditch and......'

Hope felt herself sway slightly; she thought for a moment that her legs would give way. The constable's voice sounded very far away and anyway, she didn't need this detail. There was only one thing she wanted to know but was too terrified to ask.

'Where is he?' This was the closest she could get to the crucial question.

'He's been taken to the County Hospital.' The policewoman paused. 'His injuries are quite serious. We can take you there now, if you like?'

Hope almost fell to her knees in relief. He was alive. Thank god, he was alive.

'Yes please.' She grabbed her coat and opened the door, willing the two PCs to hurry. She just wanted to get to the hospital as quickly as possible and to be with Laurie.

The slamming of car doors in the quiet neighbourhood had Josie peeking through the curtains to see Hope getting into the back of a police car before it drove off at speed. And she noticed that Laurie's car still hadn't returned.

At 12:10am Hope, at last, allowed herself to leave the intensive care unit to get herself a coffee. She'd told herself if nothing terrible had happened by midnight, he would be OK. Everything would be OK. But out in the corridor, it immediately felt wrong to be away from Laurie for even a second. She sipped the scalding hot coffee as quickly as possible - it didn't help that her hands were still shaking.

She had listened, almost without breathing, to the doctor's initial report when she arrived at the hospital. Laurie had severe leg and back injuries but as yet it couldn't be confirmed if there was any permanent damage. At the moment, the medical team were more concerned with the bang to his head which had caused concussion.

She returned now to Laurie and sat staring into space, still trying to process all the information. Gently, she stroked his hand and simply watched him as he slept.

Despite not wanting to leave his side, Hope felt the pull of something she knew she had to do but first she needed to psyche herself up - for the task of phoning her daughter. Once again, she left the room, aware that perhaps she'd already put it off longer than she should have. It was just too awful to have to give news like this over the phone, and from so far away.

Hope couldn't help a sense of relief when Sara didn't answer; it would give her a little more time to get herself together, and hopefully in a little while she would have something more positive to say. She left a brief, fairly vague message, asking her daughter to call back as soon as she could.

The eerie and timeless silence of the ICU was torturous. Another hour passed of staring at her husband's sleeping body, stroking his unmoving hand and willing him to hang in there. A nurse came along and attempted to persuade her to go home to rest. She explained that they did not expect any change to his condition in the next few hours and then she ran through the well-known clichés that Hope felt she had heard many times before although in reality she never had. The nurse told her she needed to look after herself and rest, ready for when her husband woke up. And that she'd be of no use to anyone if she was half exhausted herself.

After the safety of the bright hospital lights and its busyness, the darkness of the car park seemed to swamp her in fear and loneliness. She scanned the area to locate the taxi rank and rummaged in her bag for her phone. Still no call-back from Sara.

As she walked towards the taxis, she assured herself there was no-one else she needed to phone. Laurie's father was dead, and his mother lived in a nursing home, being in the later stages of dementia, and struggling more and more to remember who he was each time he visited. His only brother lived in America, and they hadn't seen each other or even spoken for years.

Her own sister, Emma, would be shocked to hear of Laurie's accident and would be there in an instant to offer comfort and support, but she lived down in the depths of Cornwall, hours away. And as much as Hope would love to hear her warm voice right now, there was no point ringing her in the middle of the night.

Her mother would get into a terrible state on hearing such bad news and again there was nothing to be gained from disturbing her right now. She decided to put it off for as long as she could.

A mercifully quiet taxi driver drove her home in silence. It was a swift ride, hardly any cars on the road in the village. Inside, the house was quiet as always, but in a different way. Not in a peaceful, relaxing, quiet-village-life way - it was deathly quiet, the atmosphere heavy with dread. This is what it might be like. All the time. If anything happened to Laurie, nothing would ever feel the same again.

Hope noticed she'd left the kitchen light on earlier. Not wanting to be in the dark, she left it on now and went through to the living room, closed the curtains and flicked on a couple of table lamps; their soft glow offering a little comfort. She stepped out of her shoes, took off her coat and lay down on the settee tucking her legs up tight. The room was cold, and she pulled her coat over her, comforted by her own warmth still inside. Less than a minute later she felt a gentle thud beside her as Lulu landed and found a way underneath the coat, snuggling into Hope's chest.

She thought of Laurie, lying there in hospital all alone. Tears trickled sideways down her face as she held Lulu close to her, suddenly thinking of Josie's bible. 'Please god,' she whispered. 'Please god, let him live.'

Chapter 5

'Josie!'
Ross was calling her from upstairs.
'Josie'!
She was cooking his break-fast and he was very particular about how he liked his poached eggs. She turned the gas down a little and ran out to the hallway, calling up to the galleried landing.

'What did you say? I couldn't hear you.'

Again, she heard muffled grumblings and ran up the stairs to their bedroom where Ross was still getting dressed.

'What is it? I was in the kitchen; I couldn't hear you.'

A couple of shirts had been thrown onto the bed. Ross pointed at them then turned away to take a tie from the wardrobe.

'I was just asking if there was something wrong with the iron, that's all.'

'What? No, there's nothing wrong with it. Why?'

'My shirts still have lots of creases in them. I thought perhaps the iron is broken.'

Ross was still adjusting his tie as he walked past her, out of the room.

'Is break-fast ready?'

Ross left for work after commenting that his poached eggs were a little overdone. It was Saturday and not unusual for Ross to go into his office for the morning, but Josie didn't mind, despite being on her own all week.

She waved him off from the front door, returning inside, shaking her head and smiling; her husband had these funny, grumpy moods occasionally. He'd taken his time getting out and she didn't dare hurry him, but there was something she needed to do.

This was usually the time when she and Hope had the chance to catch up. She was planning to pop over later to wish her a good holiday but after seeing the police car outside last night and then much later, Hope arriving home in a taxi, Josie was anxious to get over there as soon as possible.

She peeked through the net curtains in the living room which looked directly out onto the front of Hope's house. Despite the tall hedging, she could see that the curtains were open upstairs, but the living room curtains were still drawn and there was a light on. All rather odd. She decided to leave it a little while longer before heading over.

And in the meantime, she needed to make a start on what felt like one hundred and one chores she had to do before Ross returned home for lunch. She didn't ever want to sound ungracious but living in such a big house was all very nice apart from the huge amount of time it took to keep it clean and tidy. She would never complain; looking after their enormous home was much more enjoyable than working in a supermarket but most of the time it actually felt like a full-time job - taking care of house and husband. And she was never entirely sure if what she was doing was good enough.

Ross was going away soon for a week - up to Scotland for a golfing holiday. He said it was a business trip and would be mostly men and that she wouldn't enjoy it. Josie agreed; she didn't fancy a week in freezing cold Scotland watching him play golf, but she would need to thing about getting his things ready and packed for the trip. And while he was away, she would be able to get ahead with jobs around the house and hopefully catch up with her family, perhaps invite them over for dinner. It was a shame Hope would still be away at the same time. She hoped she wouldn't be too lonely with everyone away at once.

Hope woke up, immediately re-living the events of yesterday evening which led to why she was sleeping on the settee. Slowly, she uncurled her stiff cold limbs from under her coat, disturbing Lulu who ran to the kitchen ready for food. She wished now that she'd made the effort to go to bed last night.

As she poured some biscuits into the cat's bowl, she realised how hungry she was herself and immediately felt guilty for even thinking about food before knowing how Laurie was.

She phoned the hospital and got through to the appropriate person quicker than expected and just as the nurse had said last night - there had been no change which was conveyed as a good thing.

Hope filled the kettle and switched it on, put two slices in the toaster and then sat down at the kitchen table with her mobile in hand, taking a deep breath as she dialled Sara's number. Again, no answer and so she left another message, this time giving just a few specifics about her dad's accident. Less than two minutes later, Sara phoned back.

'Mum! What's happened? Is Dad OK?'

'Yes darling, I think so. He's still in intensive care but he's had a comfortable night.'

'You think so? What does that mean? What happened? Who was driving?'

She'd like it to be me, Hope thought instinctively. If I was driving, this could all be my fault. I'd be the one to blame.

'I wasn't in the car darling. We don't really know what happened yet. We can talk later. Are you coming down?'

'Of course I am!' Sara was abrupt and her mother's measured pause and polite response said she was forgiven but only because of the circumstances.

'I'll make a bed up for you.'

Sara relented a little. 'Thanks Mum. I'll drive straight down, and I'll be with you this afternoon.'

They said their good-byes and Hope trusted that her daughter would be sensitive and at least make an effort to keep her anger towards her below the surface for this visit. She could really do with some family support right now and was in no mood to placate a twenty-two-year-old who still suffered with teenage mood swings. She closed her eyes, as if to close down her thoughts. She shouldn't be thinking this way about her daughter, especially at a time like this.

The toast popped up behind her, making her jump, but she'd already lost her appetite. Instead, she quickly made a cup of tea and took it upstairs. Her priority now was to shower and change and get back to the hospital.

She wandered into the guest bedroom and the sight of her open suitcase still on the bed hit her like a slap in the face. Her eyes stung with tears and in an instant she was crying with full force. How could she ever have planned to go away on a holiday without Laurie? What was she thinking? She was horrified with herself.

Hope just about heard a slight knock on the front door and knew instinctively who it was. Josie, dear Josie. She ran down the stairs into the hallway. For a split second the image of the two young PCs on the other side of the door flashed into her mind but the mass of curly blonde hair and bright red scarf tied in a big floppy bow as a headband confirmed it was definitely Josie on the doorstep.

She opened the door and managed a smile for her friend. Josie smiled back; head cocked questioningly to one side. Her look said it all; I saw you go off in a police car last night. And here you are in yesterday's clothes looking like you've hardly slept, and you've been crying too.

Josie didn't wait to be invited in. She was in the hallway in a second and Hope immediately fell against her. Josie held her tight, a little overwhelmed to see her usually calm friend so distraught. In between sobs she managed to identify the words Laurie and car accident and that he was in hospital and it was serious.

Practicality kicked in and Josie settled Hope in the living room and made two large mugs of coffee. Seeing the cold toast in the toaster, she put an assortment of biscuits on a plate and when she returned to the living room, Hope's sobbing had subsided a little as she mopped her eyes and nose with a ball of tissues.

'Thanks,' she whispered, sipping some coffee. They sat in silence for a few moments.

'Do you know how long he'll be in hospital for?'

Hope shook her head, tears free-falling down her face again. It was the first time she'd repeated the doctor's words out loud, and she flinched at the sound of them. 'He has serious back and leg injuries. And concussion. They're worried about possible damage to his brain.' She swallowed and sobbed at the same time which turned into a noisy hiccough. Josie was at her side in an instant, perching on the arm of the chair, gently comforting her friend.

'He's in and out of consciousness and they're doing more tests today.'

'If there's anything I can do, anything at all you need help with, you know that, you just ask me.'

Hope smiled wryly. As if Josie had a single spare second in the day when she wasn't running around after her husband.

Suddenly Josie noticed the British Airways folder of tickets on the table beside Hope.

'Oh, your lovely holiday.'

Hope glanced at the tickets.

'I suppose you'll have to cancel? Do you want me to deal with it? I expect the last thing you want is to have to sort all that out today.'

Hope was staring into space, deep in thought.

'Hope? Can I do anything to help?'

'Yes. Actually, you can.' She looked up into Josie's expectant face. 'Go in my place,' she whispered.

'What was that?' Josie leaned in closer, hoping she hadn't heard correctly.

'Go to Bali. Take my place. Please Josie, you must.' Hope was up and out of her seat. She took a wallet folder from the desk drawer and sat back down, pulling a glossy brochure and other leaflets out to show Josie, babbling incoherently and crying at the same time.

'Hope, I can't just leave everything and go. Not today, just like that.'

'Yes, you can. Didn't you say Ross is going away soon? On a golfing holiday or something?'

'Yes, he is, but only for one week. He's not away for six weeks. He'd go mad if I went away for that long.'

'Well, just go for two then, or one. It's an open ticket. Please go. You'd love it. You might not think so, but you will. Go, and tell me what it's like. Email me and phone me and tell me all about it.' Hope was crying and at the same time smiling with enthusiasm at her idea.

Josie glanced at the brochure cover. It did look beautiful, lush tropical forests in every shade of green. Turquoise skies and brilliant sunshine. And it seemed so important to Hope who appeared near hysterical with emotion.

'OK,' said Josie. 'I'll go.' She heard her words out loud but couldn't quite believe they'd come out of her own mouth. She was relieved to see Hope immediately quieten and breathe what appeared to be a sigh of relief. This really did mean a lot to her and for Josie, there was no going back now.

Chapter 6

Hope made her way to the ICU, the hospital surroundings appearing strangely familiar to her already. It was unnerving not to recognise any of the nursing staff, but she was taken in hand with as much warmth and compassion as those of last night.

Again, she sat with Laurie, not really knowing what to do. It felt strange speaking to him, not knowing whether he could hear or not.

'Hello love, it's me, back again,' she said quietly, feeling a little awkward, knowing she would get no response. She hadn't been there long before she was asked to wait outside while the doctor attended to him.

Praying for good news, Hope watched the minutes pass painfully slowly on the clock, wondering if a lengthy doctor's visit was a good sign or not. The doctor finally emerged from Laurie's room and in the interim few seconds it took for him to reach Hope, she studied his face searching for a clue of what was to come. But it seemed as if he were practiced in giving nothing away. Or maybe he was simply tired and thinking about the rest of his busy day.

It was all good news; there was no damage to his brain, and he was expected to be fully conscious soon. And all being well, he would be transferred to a normal ward within a day or two after that. But from then on, the doctor warned, it would be a long haul back to recovery and they were still unable to say how full that recovery would be.

What they could say with absolute certainty was that Laurie would need a lot of rehabilitation and aftercare both medically and at home. The doctor assured her they would discuss things further as they progressed and then he headed off up the corridor to attend to other patients, leaving Hope alone to take it all in.

Buoyed up by the fact that Laurie would soon be fully awake, she returned to his room.

'Wonderful news Darling; you're going to be absolutely fine. Properly awake soon and then out of here and into a normal ward.'

She stayed with him for the remainder of the morning, venturing out twice to get coffee from the machine. She found it a little easier now to speak to him despite knowing he wouldn't answer.

She rested her hand on his arm and quietly told him all about Josie taking her place by going to Bali later that day.

'Josie asked me if there was anything she could do to help. I don't think she imagined for one second that I'd ask her to go in my place. And I have to say, I couldn't believe that she agreed to go. It was all a bit surreal.'

Hope pulled her chair as close to the bed as she could and carefully slid her hand under his, giving it a gentle squeeze. She knew he was in a semi-conscious state, but she wondered, all the same, if perhaps somewhere in the depths of his brain he could hear her. Perhaps sub-consciously everything she was saying was being heard and recorded.

'Yes, so Josie is off to Bali this afternoon. I wonder what Ross will say to that. God, I hope he doesn't give her too much of a hard time. She does everything for him, I wonder how he will cope!' She sighed. She hadn't had the chance to think much about the fact that in a few hours Josie would be on her way to a Wellbeing Retreat halfway around the world.

'I reckon she'll come back a changed woman. I don't think she's ever sat still for more than ten minutes – in her life.'

Hope momentarily glanced away from Laurie's face, noticing that her boots could do with a polish. Just for a second, she yearned for her holiday and grieved for all that thinking time she was losing out on but then her eyes locked on to all the medical equipment and monitors to the side of Laurie's bed and she was brought sharply back to reality.

All that mattered was that Laurie was OK, back to full health and home again. Bali would still be there and perhaps they could go together one day. There was no way she was ever planning a holiday on her own again.

She wanted to tell him all this, that she wasn't bothered about not going to Bali and they would book a holiday together as soon as he was better – wherever he wanted to go. With the hope that somehow he was able to hear her, she continued.

'Funny, it seemed exciting at the time, but now I know I wouldn't want to be away from home for six weeks – or from you. We'll book something together when you're home. It'll give us something to look forward to, something to aim for.'

Suddenly she ran out of words; it was draining, trying to keep up a one-sided conversation.

Her stomach rumbled, sounding extra loud in the silence of the room. She checked the time then stood and pushed the chair back in its place against the wall, retrieving her handbag from the floor.

She leaned over and gently stroked his forehead, hoping the warmth of her hand would send some extra healing power inside him where his body was already fighting to repair itself. In a whisper, she told him about Sara, already on her way down, and that they would both be along to visit later in the day. Finally, she kissed him on the forehead and as she got to the door, glanced back over her shoulder, acknowledging within her a definite lift in spirits – affirming to herself that everything was going to work out just fine.

Chapter 7

Josie had no idea what to pack for a luxury wellbeing spiritual retreat in Bali. She'd very quickly flicked through the masses of information Hope had given her, discovering that it would be hot there now and still quite humid too, although the rainy season had officially finished.

For some reason, she doubted that it would be a bikini-wearing sort of place and so she just packed sensible t-shirts and sundresses, jeans and walking shoes.

She'd never had to pack for a holiday at such short notice either but managed it just by aiming clothes and magazines and toiletries randomly into her suitcase, hoping that the eclectic mix would provide for all her needs.

It didn't help that she didn't feel any real excitement about the trip – least of all the eighteen-hour flight. How bizarre to be going on a holiday to Bali as a favour to a dear friend. She'd already decided to stay for one week only – that helped a little. But there was still the dreaded moment of having to explain it all to Ross.

She'd spent the morning frantically cleaning and tidying the house; put fresh sheets on the bed and tackled the pile of ironing, giving extra special attention to Ross's shirts. And for later, she was planning his favourite Saturday lunch of steak and all the trimmings. She would cook it just the way he liked it which would hopefully pave the way for a show of compassion and understanding from her husband.

Unfortunately, Ross wasn't at all happy for Josie to be disappearing for a week by herself. She didn't want to cause an argument by directly pointing out that he was going on a golfing holiday all by himself and so instead she cleverly mentioned that she would be back just in time before he left for his week in Scotland.

He begrudgingly conceded that Hope was currently going through a nightmare – and poor Laurie, a decent bloke – would of course want his wife at his hospital bedside. But Ross couldn't see why Josie had agreed to go halfway around the world in order to experience Hope's holiday for her. He disparagingly informed her that the place would be full of deep-thinking hippies who would want to discuss the meaning of life and things like that – it was hardly her sort of thing he told her.

Josie let him voice his opinion, knowing he'd soon run out of things to say. He needed to have his moan; she knew that. He liked the routine of their life and he was probably just a bit miffed because it had been sprung on him at the very last minute.

Thankfully, he was now sitting quietly in front of the TV with a large whiskey while she finished cooking and dealing with the all the things she needed to get done before she left.

A huge cut of rump steak was sizzling in the frying pan, bloody buttery juices oozing from the meat. A knock at the door had her swearing under her breath, she didn't want to overcook this steak, not today of all days. As she got to the door, she could see it was Hope, probably just back from the hospital.

'Hope, how are you? Come inside – what's the news, how is he?'

'He's doing OK. Well, actually he's the same at the moment but the doctors hope to have him in a normal ward in a few days.' Immediately Hope stepped into the hallway she could smell something delicious cooking and guessed this would be a peace offering from Josie.

'Everything alright?' she whispered.

She reckoned it hadn't been plain sailing for Josie to tell her husband she was off on a little holiday later that day. Ross could be a little possessive over his wife, she'd seen that for herself on a number of occasions. In fact, she'd half expected Josie to change her mind, or more accurately, to have it changed for her. Although it was true to say she had a very stubborn streak too which had obviously won through on this occasion. Hope smiled encouragingly.

'Yes, everything's fine. Absolutely.' Hope knew there was no way Josie would betray her husband by confiding that they'd argued.

'Ok, I can tell your dinner is nearly ready, it smells gorgeous. I'll leave you to get on. I just wanted to come and wish you good luck. Have a safe journey and enjoy yourself. Have a lovely time, won't you? We'll speak soon.'

'I'll do my best.' Josie smiled as brightly as she could.

Hope gave her a tight hug and a kiss on the cheek.

'Email me when you're there and settled in.'

'OK, I will. And give my love to Laurie,' Josie whispered.

Hope smiled and nodded then stepped outside, looking back as she retuned along the path, to wave good-bye.

Back indoors, Hope picked up the post from the doormat – a catalogue from a cashmere clothing company and a letter from her publisher. In the kitchen, she threw the catalogue in the bin and opened the letter, at the same time switching on the kettle to boil.

Off the back of the kitchen was a small hallway, with a shower room to the left, the dining room straight ahead and off to the right, at the end, was her tiny writing room. She read the letter in there, it merely confirmed receipt of her latest cookery book, and then she filed it in the appropriate folder.

All her writing commitments were taken care of and Martha, her business partner, had seemed only too pleased to be in sole charge of the shop for the next few weeks. Hope sighed, at least she didn't need to worry about work for the time being which meant she could concentrate entirely on Laurie's needs.

She made herself a cup of tea and taking it through to the lounge, sank into an armchair, closing her eyes for a few seconds but acknowledging she was much too restless to sleep. She would need to keep herself busy for the rest of the afternoon until Sara arrived.

She recalled the doctor's words from earlier. The idea of Laurie being properly awake and talking to her flooded her with relief. It would be wonderful to be able to give this news to Sara. They both needed to be strong – he could be in hospital for a while. Laurie would struggle with that; the loss of his privacy and having to mingle with strangers.

She had a sudden thought - health insurance. She banged the mug down on the coffee table and was up out of her chair, standing in the middle of the room but not exactly sure where to go next. They had private health insurance, a top policy she was sure, Platinum Band or something. But what exactly did it cover? This was the sort of household administration Laurie dealt with. But surely it would cover hospital stays and the provision of a private room.

The documents would be upstairs in Laurie's study and Hope made her way to the top of the house into the small attic room that had been made into his studio. It felt strange to be up there. She was surprised to realise she hadn't visited Laurie in his room for ages. But she wasn't surprised at how neat and tidy it was; he could be a bit OCD like that. Everything had to be exactly in its place.

There were no half-finished artworks dotted around, no scribbled ideas for cartoons or anything like that. Everything was tidied away as if it was he who was going away on holiday, she thought.

She stood in the middle of the room and looked along the shelves hoping to see a folder marked 'Insurance Documents' or something similar. But the shelves were stacked full of art books and nothing jumped out at her as being to do with domestic matters.

Under the large skylight was Laurie's drawing board and just to the side of that, his desk. She looked inside three small drawers on the left side of the desk, but these simply contained his stock of sketch pads and boxes of pencils. The long slim drawer at the top of the desk was locked. As Hope rummaged through the drawers on the right, finally locating what she'd been looking for - a wallet folder marked 'Insurance' - she couldn't help wondering about the locked drawer.

She lingered at the desk, keenly looking through the policy details for information on hospital stays and private rooms, all the time with half an eye out for a small key. Finally, she found it in the pen-tidy and without pausing to think otherwise, quickly unlocked the drawer, not allowing herself time to feel guilty.

A large brown envelope lay inside with a sticky note attached saying 'Speak with Hope – before Bali.' This must be what he was calling her to the pub for. She lifted it out. It was heavy with documents. She slid them out onto the desk; a thick wad of legal-looking forms and letters all addressed to Laurie. 'By Hand' was typed in the top right corner, confirming they hadn't been posted to him.

She couldn't make them out immediately; she was both confused yet curious at the mystery, certain that all was as it should be and would become completely clear in just a second. This was apart from the fact that they had been locked away and she knew nothing of any legal dealings within their family.

There were letters from solicitors, not local, priding themselves on specialising in family matters. Was this something to do with Sara? Was she in some sort of trouble?

Hope was barely breathing, just in short shallow gasps. And then she caught sight of the words 'Petitioner' and 'Respondent' on a form. It was an application for a divorce. Who was getting divorced she wondered? And why was Laurie involved?

She opened the form and read the names, shaking her head, disbelieving. It was her own name, and Laurie's. The attic room spun as she felt her legs give way, quickly slumping down heavily on the chair before she fell. She couldn't believe it. She stared at the form, completely numb, blinking and refocusing, willing the names to change, or disappear completely. She and Laurie could never be divorced. Why would they? They were perfectly happy.

Hope quickly spread the papers out on the desk, frantic now for answers. There were pages and pages of data, tables of figures, lists of assets and details of the values of things, including earnings and pension funds. There was even a valuation of their house. Did he want to sell their home? It looked to her as though Laurie was divorcing her and not only that, he was planning to take her for everything.

With trembling hands, she put the papers back in the envelope and replaced it in the drawer, locking it and putting the key back in the pen-tidy. She felt light-headed and her legs were still weak but more than anything she wanted to get out of the room as quickly as possible.

Downstairs in the kitchen she paced up and down, tapping her hand along the length of the long kitchen table. She couldn't think straight; could hardly organise her thoughts at all. Why did Laurie want a divorce? Why? She put her hand to her chest and was alarmed at the rate of her racing heart. She forced herself to take deep, slow breaths but it made no difference. She went through to the lounge and perched on the edge of an armchair, opened a bottle of whisky, poured a generous measure, and gulped it straight down. It took her breath away, burned her throat and numbed something else which felt vaguely pleasing. She then repeated the process.

Suddenly she remembered that Sara would be arriving soon. The thought was overwhelming. How would she handle all of this? She had yet to tell her daughter the extent of her father's injuries but of course she would not be able to tell her why her mother was stinking of whisky. Now she had her own secret to keep. Mechanically, like a wooden toy, she rose from the armchair to rinse away the evidence.

Later in the afternoon with an eye out for Sara arriving, she looked out the living room window. It was a grey afternoon and had started to drizzle.

In a parallel universe, she watched the house opposite as Josie struggled with her suitcase down the front path to a waiting taxi where the driver hauled it into the boot. There was no-one to wave her off as she slipped inside. The driver banged his door shut and they drove away.

Chapter 8

Hope sat. And waited. She managed to refrain from finishing off the entire bottle of whisky despite the overwhelming urge to completely numb herself.

She'd prepared Sara's room; made up the bed, turned the radiator up and placed some fragrance sticks on the dressing table. After that she was unable to attend to anything else, having neither the focus nor the energy.

Waiting for time to pass and for Sara to arrive, she was in an almost meditative state of non-feeling and non-thinking which she clung to. To dare to step outside this circle of numbness was to risk reducing the entire sum of her life so far to a one tiny word question – why? And she was nowhere near ready for the answer to that yet.

She heard the car pull up on the drive and park behind hers and was waiting dutifully at the open front door to greet her daughter. Sara stepped inside and let her small holdall fall to the floor. With mixed feelings,

Hope acknowledged her daughter didn't intend staying long.

She had expected an emotional hug at this point, but Sara simply gave her a quick kiss on the cheek.

'How's Dad?'

Hope was lost in thought. When was the last time she and Sara had embraced? They used to; she was sure. Why and when had it stopped?

'Mum? I was asking about Dad. When can I go see him? I'd like to know exactly what happened.'

'Whenever you're ready darling. We can go anytime.'

'Well, I'm ready now. Let's go. It's what I've driven all this way for.'

Hope wished she could tell Sara to go on her own but how on earth could she explain that she didn't want to visit her husband? Only yesterday he'd been in a terrible accident, he still wasn't out of danger yet and he might never fully recover. But the last place Hope wanted to be right now was at his bedside in hospital.

Sara crouched to retrieve something from her bag – a novel by Laurie's favourite author.

Hope looked down on her daughter, her insides twisting uncomfortably, as it occurred to her with increasing frequency that she didn't like her very much.

'I brought this up for Dad; he said ages ago he wanted to borrow it. It'll give him something to do while he's stuck in hospital.'

'That's very sweet of you. But darling, you'd better prepare yourself. He's still in a bad way. He hasn't fully regained consciousness yet and you won't actually be able to talk with him, not today anyway. It's going to be a slow road back.'

Sara looked past her mother into the kitchen, as if someone were going to appear to contradict her.

'But you don't actually know that. I mean, no-one does. Even the doctors, they don't always know what's going to happen, not for sure. Dad might just get perfectly better, and surprise all of you.'

Sara grabbed her bag and ran upstairs to her room.

Hope sighed, weary beyond measure. It was almost inconceivable that her daughter would use what had happened to Laurie to jab at her. She wasn't sure how much more she could tolerate from Sara, but she did know that she was very near the line.

Sara came back down the stairs. 'Shall we go? Are you going out like that?'

Hope looked down at herself, perfectly smart in jeans and a thick black roll neck sweater. She looked Sara directly in the eye, not trusting herself to speak a word.

'I was only thinking, just because Dad's asleep, doesn't mean we shouldn't make an effort.'

'Sara, I am tired and still in shock over what's happened. I'm doing my best here to keep it together. Your father won't care what I'm wearing.'

Sara was just about to hit back with another smart comment.

'Believe me Sara. He won't care. Now bring your keys, you're driving.'

Hope relished the silence in the car for the short drive to the hospital, but Sara's sulky silence continued all the way up to the intensive care unit.

Sara noticed the gentle rapport between her mother and the nurses; a little put out that she wasn't particularly introduced, although she was sure they would take notice of her once she'd been here a few more times.

She followed her mother into the ICU, desperate to get to her father but at the foot of the bed she faltered, stopped dead in her tracks. Hope wished now she had taken the initiative to prepare her more fully for what she saw before her. Her father was lying motionless, his eyes closed, surrounded by a tangle of wires and tubes, high-tech screens flashing an assortment of readings and measurements. She stepped forward to comfort her, but Sara was already pulling a chair next to the bed. She sat down, placing her hands gently on her father's arm.

'Dad, it's me. It's Sara.'

Hope was just about to explain that Laurie wouldn't be able to hear her, and that the idea wasn't to try to wake him up. But she didn't have the energy or the patience for another spat, and anyway it might be preferable to let her chatter on and fill the silence which would let her alone with her own thoughts.

She pulled another chair from against the wall and sat behind Sara at the bedside. The natural thing would have been to sit on the other side of the bed so that Laurie was surrounded by his family, but Hope wasn't sure what she would feel when she next looked at the man in the bed. So far, she had managed to avoid it.

She sat down and finally forced herself to look at his face, actually glad on this occasion that he was sleeping and unable to read whatever might be showing on hers.

What did she feel? Nothing. She felt nothing. She was blank, a vacuum. But she was scared too. She knew this was a safety blanket, a temporary numbness to allow the reality to steadily sink in. And when it did? What then?

Sara spun around to face her mother.

'He is going to be alright, isn't he? Mum? Mum, what's wrong?'

Hope was suddenly brought back to the present, painfully aware of her daughter's vulnerability. She was still so young – she forgot that sometimes.

'Yes, darling, I have every hope.' She looked across at Laurie, resenting the very fact of him sleeping peacefully despite all the damage he was planning to cause. But she must push aside for the moment the things he was planning to do and regardless of what would happen to them in the future, he would always be Sara's dad. The look on her daughter's face just now was one of fear – she was scared, and Hope decided to focus on that.

'It's all going to be fine.' She placed her hand on Sara's back, rubbing it as though she were a little child. 'It's Ok that he's sleeping at the moment. The doctor told me, just this morning, they expect him to be fully conscious very soon. And hopefully soon after that, he should be in a standard ward. And I'm going to look into our insurance to see if I can get him into a private room – he'll like that, won't he?'

Hope had no idea why she'd said that last bit. She had no intention of doing any kindness for him at this point.

Sara smiled but she'd fallen silent. She no longer chattered to her dad, just stared at his face, her hands still resting gently on his arm.

Suddenly, a machine to her right beeped a loud warning and she jumped, snatching her hands away as if she were the cause.

A nurse came in and ushered Hope and her daughter from the room, assuring them it was nothing to worry about as she checked the monitor settings and readings. Hope led her daughter out, Sara imploring her mother's face for confirmation that her dad would be OK.

Hope grabbed her and held her close, tight, as much as anything to prevent her from seeing her face and the thoughts that might betray her.

They waited sitting side by side in the small family room. Hope suddenly noticed they were holding hands and was surprised to realise she had no idea how long they'd been there like that. Sara's hold was tight. She gazed at a box of toys across the room, the fear showing in her staring eyes.

Later that evening Hope closed her daughter's bedroom door after having pulled the bedclothes up around her, gently pushing her hair back and kissing her forehead.

All evidence of the bolshie, wannabe independent grown-up had disappeared. Her daughter suddenly needed her mother – for the time being anyway.

Hope lie in bed looking into the darkness. After a while she drifted off into a shallow sleep but soon woke again with a vague sense of Josie on her mind. She'd been dreaming. She recalled images of a busy Josie who instead of relaxing on a poolside lounger, was frantically sweeping, prodding people's feet out of the way with her broom.

Dear Josie, she should be well into her first flight by now, on her way to the connection in Hong Kong.

Now fully awake, her mind was racing off again. It was ready to explode; bombarding her with questions as she searched her soul for answers.

Just over twenty-four hours ago, she believed she had a perfectly happy marriage. And now her husband was lying critically ill in hospital with terrible injuries. In the next room her daughter was praying for her dad to pull through – to live.

Hope asked herself what she was praying for. It was the question she was too scared to answer.

Chapter 9

It was only a thirty-minute journey to Heathrow airport, but Josie arrived just within the two-hour recommended allowance before take-off. She gave a generous tip and was relieved when the sullen, sulky-looking taxi-driver sped off. She'd left another such man at home that afternoon and knew all too well that it would take much more than a tenner to appease that situation.

It was dark and raining heavy now and as she hurried into the terminal building, the bright lights hurt her eyes. Masses of people filled the huge open space, milling around the glamorous shopfronts, coffee shops and bars all competing to entice people inside.

She checked in, glad to be rid of her bulky suitcase and headed for a familiar brand coffee shop, ordering an Americano and quickly heading for the only available table over by the wall. She'd never travelled anywhere without Ross before and she felt self-conscious now sitting on her own but as she looked around at the families and couples and friends chatting noisily, she also saw several people, like her, sitting alone eating and drinking and reading.

One thing was obvious; they were all busy doing their own thing and were not the slightest bit interested in her. She sipped her coffee, feeling a little more at ease now.

Her thoughts turned to Ross at home. They often went out Saturday evenings to one of his favourite restaurants. She liked to stay in and watch DVDs together but that didn't often happen, although right now she'd rather be there with him than anywhere else, doing whatever he wanted to do.

Perhaps he would go out on his own tonight. She plucked her phone from her handbag, thinking to send a text telling him she missed him or something, but then changed her mind. He might still be brooding about her coming away and she didn't think she could cope with a stroppy text from him right now.

The coffee shop was packed, and her table was right in the line of traffic with people constantly coming and going, banging her chair with wheelie cases and baby buggies, not even pausing for a second to apologise. She finished her drink quickly and left.

Then she wandered around the shops trying to tempt herself with top quality cosmetics to cheer herself up. A perfume representative pounced on her, offering sample sprays. Josie half listened to her polished sales pitch and allowed herself to be sprayed with a couple of expensive scents, but she couldn't motivate herself to buy either of them.

She moved on to glance over counters of watches, jewellery, sunglasses and designer silk scarves, knowing she could have bought any of it. But today it just didn't have any appeal.

The first-class cabin was calm and quiet, and Josie sank down gratefully into her spacious window seat, glad to see that the one next to her was still empty. Unusually for her, she wasn't in the mood for conversation and the last thing she wanted was a chatterbox neighbour for the next thirteen hours. She watched as people filed in, patiently locating their seats, organising their things, and getting themselves comfortable for the long journey ahead, looking for all the world as though they did this often.

She'd never travelled first class before and wondered if she stood out. She imagined Hope sitting here in this seat; she'd be perfectly comfortable. She was always relaxed and at ease and could talk to anyone.

Josie sat up taller in her seat, doing a quick recce; her jeans were Hugo Boss, her bag Ted Baker and the voluminous shawl that swamped her was by Stella McCartney. She looked the part but as her husband often reminded her - you could take the girl out of Tesco….

He thought his joke was hilarious. She never quite knew what point he was making, and whether or not he was really joking.

It was warm in the cabin and as she loosened her shawl, she noticed a waft of unfamiliar perfume from the earlier sample spray. She breathed in the warm vanilla scent and wished she'd paid more attention and made a note of what it was. Finally relaxing a little, she looked about her, trying to take it all in. Despite hundreds of passengers boarding the huge aircraft, it was surprisingly calm and peaceful with gentle music softly playing. She stretched her legs out, appreciative of the general sense of spaciousness, and watched the cabin crew perform their duties with quiet, clockwork efficiency and very particular attentiveness to their first-class passengers.

She peered through the window to the activity below. It was still raining heavily, and she watched as people on the ground, togged up in all their waterproof gear, just got on with their work, with efficient ease, seemingly unperturbed by the lashing rain. Were they due to finish soon, or had their shift only just begun, she wondered?

She flicked through the in-flight magazine but couldn't concentrate on anything and tossed it aside onto the empty seat. She fidgeted and fussed with her shawl, checked inside her bag, for nothing in particular, and then remembered the mass of paperwork Hope had given her, immediately retrieving it from her bag.

She felt slightly daunted by the pages and pages of information; confirmations of various bookings, instructions on what to do and where to go at various stages of the journey. At least she had the next thirteen hours to trawl through it all.

Anyone observing would think Josie was a nervous traveller. But that wasn't it. She sighed deeply, contemplating the eighteen-hour journey ahead of her to a country she'd never had the faintest interest in visiting. In truth, she'd rather be at home, opening a bottle of Ross's favourite wine and making everything alright.

She sighed again, her thoughts leapfrogging, from stepping-stone to stepping-stone, on a continuous loop. How had she allowed Hope to talk her into this trip? Poor Hope, and poor Laurie. She hoped he'd be OK. What if something happened to Ross – she couldn't bear the thought. She'd already upset him and that felt bad enough.

Her thoughts were interrupted by a well-spoken voice welcoming everyone aboard, encouraging passengers to take their seats and of course, wishing them the best of everything. Josie grimaced; the best thing would be when she was on the return flight back to the UK. In one week's time. She'd decided for definite that she would stay in Bali for one week only.

There were many hours ahead before she even arrived, and then a whole week to get through before it was over. Finally, she rested her head back and closed her eyes wondering if she could possibly sleep for the whole thirteen hours until they arrived in Hong Kong.

Chapter 10

Hope decided to let her daughter sleep on. It would be another long day and better all-round if she got some extra rest.

And what Hope really wanted was some time to herself; some quiet time before she did battle, not only with her daughter, but with the demons in her own head.

She moved quietly about the kitchen, anxious not to disturb Sara. While waiting for the kettle to boil, she came to the conclusion that she was unfortunate enough to possess the noisiest kettle on the planet! And then she jumped as it automatically clicked off. At the same time, Sara suddenly appeared at the kitchen door.

'Mum! You're up. Why didn't you wake me?'

Hope quickly grabbed an extra mug. Last night's humble daughter had obviously left the building and original daughter from hell had returned.

'I was just about to bring you up a cup of tea. Did you sleep well?'

'Have you phoned the hospital yet?'

'Not yet darling. A cup of tea first. They'll have let us know if there's anything to worry about.'

'Anything to worry about? He's in intensive care, with broken bones and head injuries. What more could there be to worry about? I hate all that no news is good news crap. We need to find out how he is.'

'Now, Sara, let's just get one thing straight.'

'I'll do it. I'll phone them.'

Sara banged the kitchen door shut behind her and ran upstairs presumably to use her mobile phone even though there were landline phones all over the house. Hope threw a teabag in each mug and carelessly sloshed the water in. It splashed over the work surface and onto her hand.

'Bloody hell!' She slammed the kettle down, and held her hand under the cold water, gritting her teeth, feeling the ache of tension in her jaw.

She'd finished making the tea and was sitting at the table drinking by the time Sara re-appeared – rather sheepishly.

'Have you got the number for the hospital? I can't remember the name.'

Hope picked up her phone and read out the number.

'Thanks.'

For some reason, Sara disappeared into the living room to make the call and returned just a couple of minutes later. She sat at the table opposite her mother and sipped her tea. Hope looked across at her daughter, waiting. Was she really going to make her ask? Finally, Sara spoke.

'Dad's OK. Well, they said 'no change', and that he'd had a calm night.

'That's good then', said Hope, hearing the lack of conviction in her voice and moving quickly to cover it. 'Now, do you want some breakfast before we head up to the hospital or shall we get something out?'

Sara was already out of her chair, leaving her unfinished mug of tea where it was on the table.

'I think getting to the hospital should be our priority. I don't know how you can even think about food right now. I'll just grab my bag from my room.'

Hope snatched up the mugs throwing the dregs into the sink before banging them into the dishwasher and slamming the door shut.

This would have to stop. She was prepared to cut Sara a little slack, in the circumstances, but for a limited time only. And she was just about reaching that limit.

A knock at the door made Hope jump. The experience of seeing two policemen on her doorstep now had her jittery and fretful of what might happen next. She dashed into the hallway and through the frosted front door glass could see, thankfully, an ordinary-looking woman standing there. Tall and slim, it looked like Martha. She was elegant as always in a camel coat, her glossy brown hair styled in a short swingy bob.

Martha was looking back down the garden path but turned quickly at the sound of the door opening, a worried look on her face. She'd made a couple of phone calls to the house; one last night and another this morning, both unanswered.

'Oh. Hello Hope. What are you doing here? Shouldn't you be on your way to Bali?'

'Hello Martha, I'm so sorry, come on in. I really should have phoned you by now. Come in, I'll explain everything.'

Martha stayed where she was. 'No thanks, I won't come in. I was just passing, and… So, is everything OK?' Martha looked past Hope into the hallway as if she was expecting someone else to be there.

'Martha, it's Laurie; he's had a car accident. Come inside, and I'll explain, the little of what I know anyway.'

Martha stared into Hope's face, seemingly unable to speak. Finally, she stepped inside. Hope suddenly realised how unemotional and matter of fact she must have just sounded. She turned to go through into the kitchen, knowing Martha would automatically follow her, and giving her a few vital seconds to decide exactly how much she wanted to confide in her friend.

She and Martha had been good friends for about five years. They'd met at a local wine tasting event. This was something she and Laurie were particularly interested in and had made plans to visit the south of France and tour the vineyards many times, but as with so many of their plans, it had never happened. This had been a local event Hope had seen advertised and made it a belated birthday gift to Laurie.

Martha had bravely attended on her own as a means of making new friends. She was very young to be a widow, with the big 40 as her next birthday. Her husband had died after a long illness the year before.

She had since become good friends with Hope and Laurie although it wasn't so much that they had taken her under their wing – more the other way around. She would help to organise summer barbecues in their garden, and they would often go out all together for an early evening drink at the local pub.

They had immediately hit it off as they discovered shared interests in yoga and meditation, and above all a passion for anything to do with baking. Martha taught cookery at the college in town and was fascinated by Hope's writing talent. They spent afternoons together sharing recipes and ideas, Martha enthusiastically making suggestions for Hope's cookery books.

It was her idea to open the shop selling cookery equipment especially for children to go with her books, and when the shop opened three years ago, Martha was the obvious person to go into partnership with.

Recently, Hope increasingly doubted whether this had been such a good idea. It was hard work and took a lot of her time. She wondered sometimes how she'd allowed Martha to talk her into it.

As she reached the kitchen and filled the kettle, she decided not to tell Martha anything about what she'd discovered and Laurie's plans to leave her.

'Tea or coffee?' Again, she noticed the lack of emotion in her voice, and questioned herself. How should she sound, a woman in this situation? What would be normal - she had no idea. At this precise moment, she felt nothing. Hopefully, Martha would interpret her monotone simply to be the result of shock.

'Coffee please,' Martha whispered as she perched on a stool at the counter.

Hope was surprised to see the colour had drained from her face. Poor Martha, she and Laurie were good friends.

'I'm sure he'll be fine.'

'Yes, I hope so.'

Hope banged about with coffee cups and saucers, covering the ominous silence that had filled the room. She was awaiting the inevitable barrage of questions about what had happened and when Laurie would be coming home. But as yet there were none.

Finally, she carried the coffee over to Martha and sat next to her. Her friend was staring into the distance, as if trying to make sense of what she'd been told, even though in fact, it was very little.

Hope felt a little awkward; she felt the need to comfort Martha but was concerned that the only things coming to mind would sound fickle and clichéd. And really, shouldn't Martha be comforting her?

'Drink up. It's nice and strong, and sweet.'

Martha sipped the steaming coffee. She was deep in thought, a slight frown creasing her forehead and her eyes darting about the room as her mind searched for answers.

'When did it happen?'

'The day before yesterday. In the evening.'

Martha nodded, as if in acknowledgement. 'And what did happen?'

'We're not sure exactly. His car veered off the road and hit a tree.'

'But he's OK? You did say he's alright.'

'Well, we're hoping he will be. In time. He's got some serious injuries. It's a little early to tell at this stage if there'll be any lasting damage.' Again, Hope could hear the cold detachment in her voice as if she were the doctor doing the talking.

Martha almost lost grip of her cup, just managing to bring it down to the saucer with a crash. It occurred to Hope that maybe all this talk was bringing back memories of the relatively recent death of her husband. Hope placed her hand over Martha's.

'Martha, it's OK, you don't need to stay. I'm over the worst of the shock. And Sara's here with me. We'll be fine. And I know you're taking care of the shop so that's one thing I don't have to worry about.'

Just for a second, a look of relief lightened Martha's face. She slid her hand out from underneath Hope's as she eased herself off the kitchen stool, suddenly more than a little eager to escape.

'Yes of course, I'll leave you to it. You'll want to be alone with Sara. I'm glad that she's come down to be with you.' Martha knew that mother and daughter didn't get along terribly well at the moment, and she had no idea why she had just said that. She needed to leave before she said something else equally stupid.

At the front door, Hope kissed Martha's cheek. 'Thanks for coming by, I appreciate it. I'll keep you posted.'

Martha opened the door. 'Yes, please do. Tell him I called around, will you?'

'Yes, of course. I'll tell him.'

Martha walked back to her car and Hope closed the door, standing in the hallway for a few seconds slightly baffled by the visit.

Sara came down the stairs. 'Who was that?'

'Martha.'

'Oh, someone told her about Dad then?'

'No actually. She didn't know. I just told her. She was completely shocked.'

'Oh, right. What was she calling for then?' Sara was rummaging in her untidy sack of a handbag, her head almost entirely inside.

Hope looked from one side of the hallway to the other as if expecting the answer to this simple question to leap out at her, before she had to, rather sheepishly, answer. 'I don't actually know.'

Sara came out of her handbag and looked at her mother as if she were a complete idiot then sniffed sharply which in itself sounded like an insult. 'Shall we go?'

Chapter 11

Sara and Hope arrived at the hospital to the news that Laurie had fully regained consciousness. However, he was currently undergoing further tests which meant they wouldn't be able to visit him until later. Sara was deflated with disappointment and at the same time jubilant to hear that her dad was conscious again. Hope simply felt relief that she wouldn't have to face talking to Laurie – just yet.

The nurse had picked up on Sara's disappointment and addressed her directly.

'It's very encouraging. All results so far are good. But the downside is that he will be very tired, and it's important to let him rest.'

'Would it be better if we came back tomorrow?' Hope suggested, hoping she didn't sound as desperate as she felt. She could sense Sara's angry face turned towards her.

'It's up to you but he would benefit from being allowed to sleep.'

'OK, we'll come back tomorrow.'

Sara waited until they'd left the busy hospital and were walking across the car park.

'Why did you say that Mum? We could've gone back tonight.'

'You heard what the nurse said, you don't want to interfere with your dad's recovery do you?'

That was a cheap shot, and Hope knew it. But it did the trick of silencing Sara's protests and delayed the prospect of her having to talk to Laurie for another twenty-four hours.

'It is good though, isn't it Mum? That we'll be able to see him properly awake tomorrow?'

'Yes dear, it is.'

'And we'll be able to talk to him at last. I wonder what he'll remember about the accident and what happened.'

'Yes, I wonder that too.'

Tomorrow, Hope would have to speak to her husband for the first time since she'd discovered that he was planning to divorce her, and in the process, attempt to ruin her business and livelihood. Would he even remember that he had called her to the pub on the night of the accident, no doubt to give her this terrible news?

Tomorrow, she would look into the eyes of the man she had been married to for over twenty years and she would know if he remembered – immediately.

'And just think, he could be home soon. Won't that be great? We can care for him ourselves, we ought to tell the hospital that, let them know that we can help him with whatever he needs to get him fully recovered. Can't we? Eh, Mum?'

'Yes, darling. Of course we can.'

But Hope was thinking that it would be her and her alone who would be left with the responsibility of caring for Laurie. Sara would go back to wherever it was she was secretly hiding. Oh yes, she would visit regularly and bring gifts of favourite chocolates and books and magazines. She would sit and chat with her dad, make him laugh and love her, and he would indulge her while Hope, behind the scenes, would be doing all the real, hard work. She didn't know if she could do it.

It was starting. The bitterness. Hope acknowledged the actual moment as she calmly closed the car door, starting the engine and driving away, out of the hospital car park.

As she pulled onto the drive, Sara leapt out and unlocked the front door, hopefully to go into the kitchen to make a drink. Hope was desperate for a decent cup of coffee.

In the hallway, she closed the front door with all the weariness of someone who'd just run a marathon – she was ready to drop. Sara had already disappeared upstairs and in the kitchen, no evidence of a cup of coffee being made for her. She took two mugs and filled the kettle and simply stood where she was until it boiled.

Sara suddenly appeared in the kitchen; her overnight bag dropped at her feet.

'OK, I'm off to Gemma's. I'm staying with her tonight. Catching up on stuff and everything.'

Hope nodded, as Sara helped herself to a couple of biscuits from the tin on the dresser behind her. It was easier to lie when you didn't have to look the other person in the face. But then Hope couldn't stop herself.

'I didn't realise you still kept in touch with Gemma. Do you see her often?'

'Yeah, now and again. You know how it is.'

Hope turned to face her daughter already back at the kitchen door, picking up her bag.

'OK, see you tomorrow Mum. I'll be back in the morning.' She allowed herself one fleeting glance at her mother – the safety of space between them, before she turned and left the house.

Hope put one mug back on its tree, made herself a strong coffee and sat down at the table, holding her head in her hands – her head felt like a ton weight, and her arms weren't strong enough to carry it.

She closed her eyes briefly, acknowledging that actually the rest of the day would be easier with Sara out of the way. And although she was positive, she wasn't spending the night with Gemma, she wasn't going to waste any energy today trying to figure out where she would be and who she would be with. Those lies could wait. Today she would decide how to deal with her husband's lies and whether or not she would allow him and them back into her home.

Chapter 12

Hong Kong airport appeared completely overwhelming to Josie at first. She felt panicked at the foreignness of the place but there was no escape and no option other than to try to keep calm and pay attention to where she needed to be. As it turned out, getting through the airport was a breeze and without any further anguish she found herself boarding the connecting flight to Bali.

In three hours, she'd finally be there and after she'd dutifully listened to the safety demonstration, she looked ahead to arriving at Denpasar. It was probably nothing at all like Hong Kong airport; she imagined a shaky wooden shack and a lone attendant at passport control – stamping passports with a rubber stamp and ink pad.

As a contrast to the luxury and spaciousness of the British Airways first class flight, this aircraft was crammed full and now that they had landed, having the window seat meant she had to wait for her neighbours to move first. Instinctively she turned to peer through the window, squinting into the darkness trying to make out the landscape.

She was finally exhausted of air travel. It was hot and stuffy and even though the aircraft doors were open, there was no relieving waft of a refreshing breeze. Josie felt bedraggled and in need of a shower and was very tired.

Through the window, she was surprised to see the bright lights of a large, very modern terminal building. Not a shaky shack in sight.

This time next week she would be on her way home – the thought of it made her smile, but right now she was eager to get off the plane, step out into the balmy air of that tropical evening and find out exactly what she'd let herself in for.

Beginning to feel like a seasoned traveller, she followed the other passengers off the plane and into the airport. Among the paperwork she'd studied earlier, she'd found confirmation of a booking of the airport premier VIP service.

On arrival, she was to be met by a member of staff who would be holding a sign with her name on. Josie assumed this would still be in the name of Hope Clements but was amazed to see a sign bearing her own name, Josie Bell, held by an assistant who greeted her warmly and welcomed her to the island.

From there she was fast-tracked through the Visa paperwork and immigration clearance. A porter collected her luggage before she was escorted through customs, and finally they left the coolness of the air-conditioned terminal building and stepped out into the warm night air where she was introduced to her driver for the three-hour scenic journey from the airport to Singaraja.

Feeling comfortable and relaxed, and very well looked after already, she settled into the back of the taxi acknowledging for the first time, the slightest twinge of excitement at the prospect of what was to come. She looked out the window, curious for her first viewing of Bali but it was dark out and she was suddenly overcome by tiredness, having only slept in fits and starts throughout the journey. She rested her head back, closed her eyes and fell asleep within seconds, sleeping for most of the journey to The Harmony Wellbeing Retreat.

Josie had been rocked to sleep for the last three hours, waking occasionally, confused at first before remembering where she was. The sensation of the car coming to a complete stop woke her fully, although the driver had already retrieved her luggage and stacked it neatly outside before she had even got out of the car.

Even at this hour of the night he smiled effusively as he held the door open for her. She tried to return the gesture but couldn't summon the energy for anything more than what felt like a silly grin. Her legs felt like lead and her head was groggy; she felt as though she'd been dragged from her bed.

As she walked towards the reception building, she heard the car start and turned to see it speeding back along the driveway, presumably returning to the airport. Turning back, as if by magic, a young woman had appeared, welcoming her up the steps into the reception pavilion, a large wooden structure, open on all sides to the tropical night. She was pretty, bright eyed and smiling, making Josie feel as if she were a hundred years old. She introduced herself as Dewi to which Josie nodded before introducing herself. And then she felt rather silly, of course she would know who she was, she was expecting her.

Trying desperately to focus and concentrate on what Dewi was saying, she tried to shake off the awful feeling of being drugged up and at the same time, hungover.

Dewi smiled a concluding smile and picked up a folder of information before leading Josie out of the pavilion and along a softly lit narrow pathway pulling Josie's suitcase behind her.

Within minutes, they were inside what was to be her home for the next week. Dewi said something about having a good sleep and that she should phone reception if she needed anything at all. Breakfast would be served to her at nine o'clock on the terrace. She left, still smiling, closing the door so quietly behind her as if she knew Josie was already asleep – on her feet.

Josie pulled her suitcase into the bedroom and smiled at the four-poster bed dressed in pure white bedlinen with muslin drapes tickling in the soft breeze.

She took a bottle of mineral water from her bag and drank a little. Then she took out her phone and sent

Ross a text message saying she'd arrived safely, sending him her love and lots of kisses.

Next, she stepped out of her shoes, threw her shawl aside and fell back blissfully onto the bed.

Chapter 13

Sitting at the kitchen table, having drunk two cups of strong coffee and now a cup of tea, Hope gazed out the window at heavy grey skies and the tops of the conifers being whipped by the wind. All being well, Josie should have arrived in Bali by now. There would be no grey skies there or chilly winds. Hope sighed and felt a shiver of resentment run through her, immediately berating herself – she'd practically bullied her into going.

Sundays used to mean a walk around the lakes followed by roast dinner and then a lazy afternoon watching old movies. Hope wallowed in her memories, then felt an uncomfortable reality check as she tried to remember the last time she'd cooked a Sunday roast. It was a long time ago. She'd taken to working at the weekends and she and Laurie had started going to the local pub for their Sunday lunch. That had soon become the norm but then that had fallen away too.

With Sara out of the way, supposedly at Gemma's, she'd thought some quiet time to herself was exactly what she needed. She'd be able to try, at least, to clear her head and organise her thoughts – two seemingly simple things which felt like impossible tasks. But now, she felt the whole afternoon and evening stretching out endlessly before her.

Sipping lukewarm tea, she attempted to sort the chaos in her mind into some semblance of order. But she just couldn't do it. She was immobilised – both mentally and emotionally, and also physically. It was as if she was stuck to the chair. But if she were to get up, she knew exactly where she would go. It was much safer to stay put.

In the early evening after a feeble half-hearted attempt at a bowl of soup for dinner, Hope finally left the kitchen. Despite good intentions to do something constructive and regardless of the severe warnings she'd given herself, still she went upstairs, heading for the top of the house.

Moving slowly onto the first landing, Hope paused. She pushed the door open to the guest bedroom. For a moment, the sky had cleared, and a beam of bright spring sunshine fell across the room. Her suitcase lay where she had left it, on the bed, still open and ready to squeeze the last few things inside at the last moment.

Only two days ago, she'd been ready to finally set off on her dream holiday – something she'd planned for over six months. She'd been so happy, hardly able to believe it was happening at last. And then it had been cruelly snatched from her. She slammed the suitcase shut. And then slapped her hand down on it hard. And then again, and again, and again, her palm stinging more with each slap. It wasn't fair; what had she done to deserve all this?

Much more purposefully now, she marched up the narrow winding stairway that recessed into the wall and which took her directly into Laurie's study/workroom. She stood still, taking a deep breath, trying to calm it and her thoughts and mostly her actions as she felt an over-whelming desire to tear the room apart.

She wanted to rip his framed artwork from the walls and smash them to the floor, to pull all his neatly stored folders out and empty them into a messy pile and take his expensive hard back art books and beat them and break them until they were ruined.

Hope placed her hand over her mouth and closed her eyes as if this could silence her thoughts. Her breath was too quick, and she felt light-headed.

She sat down at Laurie's desk - exactly where she knew she would be sitting as soon as she walked back into this room.

Like a robot, she reached for the key in the pen-pot, unlocked the narrow drawer immediately below the desktop and took out the envelope full of documents. She could feel her pulse racing again and sat for a moment simply staring at the envelope.

Finally, she emptied the contents onto the desk, a lot more than she remembered, and began sifting through them, slower and more deliberate this time, taking it all in and trying to work out exactly what it might mean for her. There was the house valuation; copies of bank statements going back over many years; copies of their pension documents and a few financial investments they'd made, mostly after Hope's grandmother had died and left her a little money. At the bottom of the pile was the actual divorce petition. Hope leaned forward, resting her elbows on the desk for support, and began reading.

Laurie was citing irreconcilable differences as his reason for wanting a divorce. He had made an extensive list of what he considered to be their differences and Hope read through them all, her pulse racing again, and her breath shallow, barely able to believe what she was reading.

He made a reference to her unreasonably long working hours that went late into the evenings and weekends. How dare he? It was these long hours that allowed him to play around drawing cartoons all day and not having to get a proper job.

He also referred to the fact that they hadn't been away on holiday, not even a weekend away to visit their daughter at university. Hope nodded her head as if in time to a beating drum. The response to that accusation went along the lines of opening his eyes to the truth by challenging the constant deception and lies from his precious daughter who wasn't even at university anymore.

The list went on; Hope couldn't help a wry smile at all his petty grievances. There was an iota of satisfaction to be gained from the obvious fact that really, he had very little to complain about.

But then the last entry on the list did hit hard. Laurie stated that the physical side to their relationship was non-existent and had been for years.

Hope felt it like a blow to her belly. She doubled over, clutching herself, in the chair. How could he discuss the most private and intimate part of their relationship with a stranger? It was as if he were scoring points against her. As if it were a business deal.

Hope straightened herself in the chair, putting her hand to her mouth again, noticing this time that her hand was shaking.

And anyway, all of this was complete nonsense, totally fabricated to ensure he got his own way, for whatever reason he felt he had. She shook her head as if to confirm none of it was true, but at the same time she was trying to recall the last time they had made love. She couldn't remember the actual day. But it wasn't so long ago. She was sure of it. She shook her head again, dismissing the thought. Her mind was simply too jumbled to think straight – she'd be able to think more clearly later and then she'd easily remember. Damn him for making her justify herself in this way. What could he be hoping to gain from humiliating her like this?

The possible answer came at her like another body blow, and she couldn't believe she hadn't thought of it until now. What if he wanted to be with another woman?

Hope had no idea how long she'd been up in the attic. Back downstairs, it was dark now and she went from room to room closing the curtains with force, almost ripping them off the poles. The temperature had dropped, and she switched the heating on, turning up the thermostat at the same time.

Her anger was all-consuming but instead of a need to lash out, she revelled in a more menacing, more powerful sense of dignity and poised restrain. She would not crack, crash or be broken. She would deal with this.

Her empty insides rumbled with hunger, and she knew she ought to eat something, but even if she found the energy to cook, she would have no appetite. Taking a dry biscuit from the tin, she nibbled it to test her theory. No. It stuck to the roof of her mouth, tasteless, inedible.

In the living room, Hope was almost surprised to see Lulu curled in a ball and fast asleep on the settee. She'd almost forgotten she had a cat. When was the last time she'd been fed? Hope backtracked to the kitchen, relieved to see cat biscuits and water in their respective bowls on the floor.

She plonked herself down on the settee right next to Lulu who didn't even flinch. She was being ignored – Hope knew that – being punished for being an inattentive owner over the last few days. She stroked Lulu's head, rubbing her little ears affectionately.

The grey and white cat stood and fidgeted on the spot. Hope expected her to move across to her lap and snuggle into her but instead she jumped to the floor, stretched slowly and stalked off, obviously still in a huff.

Tears started to prick at the back of her eyes and Hope sniffed and took a deep breath, standing up to get on and do something, realising how absurd she was being. She tidied some books on the coffee table and looked about her for something else that needed doing. Her eyes came to rest on the drinks cabinet then they flitted to the clock and gave the OK that it wasn't too early for a drink.

She poured a generous measure of whiskey and topped it up with soda, snuggling herself back on the sofa, sipping her drink slowly; sip, sip, sip, without putting the glass down, until it was gone. She was still cold, the heating wasn't getting through yet, and the next glass was mostly whiskey with just a dash of soda for the sake of decency. By the third glass, she didn't bother with a mixer at all. And now her tears were freefalling, streaming down her cheeks, dropping from her jaw, soaking into her top and falling into her drink. She mopped them up with balls and balls of tissues, only for them to immediately be replaced with fresh tears.

Exhausted from crying and sleepy from the alcohol, she settled down, just for a quick nap. She pulled a throw from the back of the settee and covered herself, finally beginning to feel warm. She closed her eyes and fell asleep.

Sara drove onto the drive and parked behind her mother's car. She'd had a terrific day away and was buoyed up with renewed optimism and hope for the future – just exactly what she needed.

As she let herself into the house she was hit by a wave of stuffy heat, as if the central heating had been left on all night.

'Mum? It's me! Where are you?'

For a second Sara thought something terrible might have happened to her dad but then she remembered her mum's car on the drive, and instinctively she knew her mum would contact her immediately if there was any news. She suddenly felt a little ashamed of her behaviour over the last few days.

Perhaps her mum was out in the garden. She went through to the living room to look through the French doors and was shocked to see Hope fast asleep on the settee with a rug half-heartedly pulled across her and Lulu snuggled into her chest.

At the same time, she noticed the almost empty whiskey bottle – her mum didn't even like whiskey – the empty tissue box, surrounded by screwed up tissues obviously used to mop her tears.

'Oh Mum!' Sara was at her side in an instant, kneeling on the floor and bending to hold her.

Hope jolted awake, not immediately able to understand what was happening. She'd fallen asleep on the settee but what was Sara doing back here?

'What are you doing here?' she asked gently, uncomfortably aware of the sound of confusion in her voice.

'I said I'd be back in the morning Mum.'

'Is it morning?' Hope looked towards the French doors where the curtains were still drawn. The room was in cosy darkness apart from a single table lamp. And then she turned her head sharply towards the hallway and confirmed the light streaming in through the front door.

She held her head in her hands; memories of yesterday evening returning perfectly clear now, and her head pounding. Embarrassed at her behaviour and panicking as to how she was going to explain herself, it suddenly appeared that there would be no need as Sara drew her own conclusion – the obvious one really.

Hope swung her legs to the floor as Sara sat down close to her, pulling her mum into a hug as she put both arms around her.

'It'll all be OK. You'll see. This is going to be a great day – we're going to talk to Dad – properly, I mean. And he's actually going to be able to talk back to us this time.' Sara laughed, a little nervously, a slight, momentary frown darkening her face with the realisation that he just might not be the same, good old dad talking back to them.

'It's going to be fine. I know it is. I can feel it.'

Sara stood up, smiling at her mother. She collected all the tissues, stuffing them into the empty box, taking it and the glass out to the kitchen.

'I see you had a bit of a one-woman session last night. It's OK. Sometimes we have to do these things. I'll make us some breakfast.'

Hope sighed, and grimaced and felt relieved that her daughter wasn't giving her a hard time. Her daughter? Was that really her daughter out there in the kitchen? The young woman who'd just given her a hug, reassured her and was almost whistling with happiness? Wherever she'd been last night, and whoever she'd been with, they'd certainly lifted her spirits – and she'd stake a lot of money that it wasn't Gemma.

Hope stood and folded the throw, replacing it neatly on the back of the settee. She felt a little light-headed, lack of food and too much alcohol, she deduced. She had no idea what Sara was cooking up in the kitchen but was pretty sure she couldn't stomach a full fry-up. But she would need to eat something - she would need sustenance ready for the hospital visit later that morning and for facing the man she'd thought was her loving husband.

Her stomach flip-flopped, just at the thought of it. And the thought of Laurie brought back memories of yesterday and the time she'd spent in his workroom. She couldn't remember, had she replaced all the documents back in the drawer?

Out in the hallway, she could hear Sara in the kitchen, banging around with crockery and cutlery. Quickly, she dashed upstairs, all the way to the attic and was relieved to see that everything was tidied away, exactly as she'd found it. She quickly checked that she'd locked the drawer which she had.

She turned to go back downstairs, not wanting Sara to know she'd been up here in case she mentioned it to her father. But it was too late. As she descended the stairway, Sara was calling from halfway up the lower stairs.

'Were you up in Dad's room?'

'Yes, but not for any particular reason though.'

'Oh Mum, I know exactly how you feel. I've wanted to go in there a few times, you know, to be among his things, his drawings and that.'

Hope followed her daughter back into the kitchen.

'But I wasn't sure whether to; I know he often keeps it locked so I thought it best not to.'

Hope just managed to refrain from saying anything that might reveal her surprise and let slip that Sara had a better knowledge than she did of what went on in her own home.

And if Sara thought she was up there for sentimental reasons, she'd leave it at that too. She'd keep the real reason to herself, that was the kindest thing, for now anyway.

Chapter 14

Josie had woken several times in the night and instinctively tried to work out what time it was in the UK. Each time she was convinced she would never get back to sleep.

The first time, she'd got up and rummaged through her suitcase for a loose t-shirt which she changed into.

Later into the night, she'd wandered around the villa in the dark, not wanting to switch on a light for fear of disturbing a neighbour. Despite not being able to see anything in detail, she got the distinct impression that this was a very large villa with spacious terraces, and she wasn't absolutely sure, but thought she could make out a small swimming pool in the garden.

She awoke now to bright sunlight bouncing off the whitewashed walls. Soft, fine curtains wafted gently on the merest of a breeze. She checked her watch, it was eight o'clock, not even midnight at home. Her thoughts immediately turned to Ross.

She sat up and swung her legs to the side of the bed, hanging her head which was still groggy.

'God, I feel awful! This must be jet-lag then.'

The room was cool and yet when she stood, the smooth stone floor felt almost warm underfoot. She was thirsty and drank greedily from the bottle she'd left on the table the night before and then she picked up her phone, hoping for a message from Ross by now, but there was nothing from him.

There were, however, two messages from Hope – one from yesterday wishing her a safe journey and another one a few hours ago, asking if she'd arrived yet and asking her to let her know she was OK.

Josie went into the next room which appeared to be an open-air lounge. The walls to the side and in front of her were completely open to the terrace beyond with only a small rattan roof as protection if need be. Out on the terrace she saw that she'd been right the night before; there was a small plunge pool right in the middle of the garden for her sole use.

Suddenly her eyes filled and spilled over with tears trickling down her cheeks. She felt over-whelming sadness; Hope should be here now, enjoying this view. This was her holiday. She'd earned it, worked hard for it and now she was waiting patiently at a hospital bedside not knowing if her husband was ever going to be fully well again. It should be Hope here, not her.

And Ross really should have sent her a text message by now. She sniffed and wiped the tears away with the back of her hand, then went back inside.

After slowly and unenthusiastically unpacking her suitcase, Josie sat on the edge of the bed to send a text to Hope. At first, she simply confirmed she'd arrived safely and that all was well. But then she added more detail, letting Hope know the retreat was a beautiful place and the villa was amazing, stunning. She promised to email her soon with lots of photos and ended by sending her love to both of them.

Feeling much fresher and a little lifted in spirits after a shower, Josie was just thinking about getting something to eat when she heard a voice call out as two young women appeared on the terrace and began setting out breakfast for her. There was a selection of traditional western food including bread, ham, eggs, tea and coffee as well as an abundance of colourful exotic fruit.

One of the women reminded Josie that she had an appointment for a consultation with the retreat specialist at ten o'clock, to assess her personal health plan for the next six weeks.

Josie didn't know how to begin explaining that she wasn't the original person who made the booking or that she didn't need a personal health plan and most particularly that she would not be staying here for six weeks.

Instead, she sat at the little table on the terrace and simply nodded in agreement as it was explained to her that all she needed to do was go along to the lounge area in the main building - the best entrance for her being directly opposite the infinity pool which was just back along the pathway she'd come down last night.

Josie nodded gratefully and thanked them, silently wishing them to leave so that she could devour the food in front of her which she promptly did as if she hadn't eaten for days.

Chapter 15

Sara had cooked breakfast and Hope had been surprised at her skills. She'd cooked a full English fry-up, the way to a man's heart, she thought. Something new her daughter had obviously learnt over the last few months.

But despite the perfectly cooked food, Hope couldn't face sausage and bacon and managed to get away with pushing the food around the plate, successfully avoiding eating very much at all.

Having showered, and now towelling her hair dry, she looked in the bathroom mirror, shocked to see the worn out, old lady staring back at her. It had been years since she'd had a hangover and she also felt slightly sick but acknowledged that could be due to the impending hospital visit scheduled for later that morning.

She had left Sara happily tidying the kitchen and would have preferred to stay quietly in her room, but this was not to be.

'Mum! Coffee's here and it's getting cold!'

Oh dear, thought Hope, it sounds like the happy mood is officially over.

'Mum! Did you hear me?'

'Yes darling, I'm coming.' Hope felt weak and had no energy to fight. She tripped on the bathroom mat, very nearly smashing her head to the wall. She slammed her hands down onto the unit to save herself, sending bottles and jars crashing to the floor.

'Mum! What on earth are you doing?'

This time Hope didn't answer but muttered to herself, 'Yes, I'm fine thank you.' She steadied herself, looked in the mirror, took a deep calming breath and looked hard at her reflection. The person looking back at her seemed like a stranger; she didn't know who she was any more, what she felt or what she thought, what she wanted or what she was going to do. But somehow, she would get this difficult day over with and then it was time to start making some decisions.

Later that morning she drove them to the hospital, her mind so over-loaded, she briefly wondered if you could be fined for distracted-driving.

'Oh, I forgot to tell you,' said Sara.

'What?'

'Martha phoned. While you were in the shower.'

'Is everything OK?' Hope was automatically thinking cookery business.

'Yeah, she was just asking after Dad. And she wanted to know if she could visit. I said it was probably just family only at the moment. It was OK to say that, wasn't it?'

'Yes, of course. You're probably right.'

'And I don't suppose Dad wants to listen to Martha going on, like she does. I should think he'd actually like a break from her.'

Hope took a quick sideways look at Sara trying to fathom what she meant but she simply added the query to the queue in her head, as she returned her concentration to the task in hand – finding a parking place in the hospital car park.

Their appointment was with Dr Powell at ten-thirty. Together she and Sara walked along now familiar hospital corridors in silence. They checked in at reception and were immediately taken along to the doctor's office. As they sat down in front of his desk, he smiled up at them and without saying anything, looked back down at his notes. He breathed in deeply, noisily through his nose and straightened in his chair as if ready to give a speech.

'Okay, I'm very pleased with your husband's progress. At this point every minor step forward is a good sign even if it doesn't appear to be so. You must understand that while Laurie's injuries are no longer serious, they're not straight-forward. That is, the breaks to the bones in his leg are complicated and will need careful monitoring if he's to make a good recovery. His progress may be painfully slow not just for himself but for his family too.'

Hope felt her heart sink. How would she ever cope with this? She looked across at Sara who was nodding earnestly, hanging on the doctor's every word.

'We'll keep him with us for at least another week and will go through his recovery plan in more detail before he goes home. I just wanted to give you a heads up and prepare you for the long haul and what you may have to deal with.'

'That's fantastic,' beamed Sara. 'Isn't it Mum? Dad will be home next week.'

'Yes, yes it is, of course.' Hope felt a mild sense of relief that she had over a week before considering what she should do about having Laurie back home.

'Are there any questions from either of you at this point?'

'No, thank you,' answered Hope, her voice barely above a whisper. She looked across at her daughter, praying she had nothing to ask – she didn't think she could take any more graphic details about Laurie at the moment. Thankfully Sara was shaking her head, obviously just as keen to get out of the doctor's office, albeit for very different reasons.

'Now, I won't keep you any longer, you must be anxious to go and talk to your husband, your father.' Dr Powell looked from Hope to Sara, smiling at them both. He stood, marking the end of their meeting, the cue for them to leave and make their way to Laurie's room.

Hope's legs were made of lead. She didn't want to move. She wanted to remain in the chair, in the doctor's office, and not have to deal with what was waiting for her just down the corridor. But Sara was already over by the door, chomping at the bit to get to her father and she wouldn't be delayed.

'Come on Mum! He'll be waiting for us.'

'Yes darling, I'm coming.'

Sara led the way down the corridor, speeding along, just about able to stop herself from breaking into a run. Hope followed, trying to keep up with her daughter's pace but at the same time wanting to run in the opposite direction.

They arrived at Laurie's room together and Hope was happy for Sara to enter first. He was sitting up in bed, propped up by a mountain of pillows. Sara was at his side in an instant, plonking herself down onto the side of his bed and wrapping her arms around him, obscuring him from Hope's view for a few seconds. She took the moment to steady herself.

Finally, Sara drew back and sank into a visitor's chair at her father's side. Slowly, Hope walked closer, locking eyes with her husband, neither of them able to find any suitable words.

Hope had never known what to expect at this moment but now that it was here, the main thing that struck her was how well Laurie looked. Her world had been turned completely upside-down, but he looked exactly the same as he had just a few days before. He was her husband, familiar, kind and loving, and he was alive and well. The relief of it weakened her legs and she thought for just a second she was going to collapse to the floor, quickly managing to steady herself by holding onto the edge of the bed.

Laurie looked up at her expectantly. She knew she had tears in her eyes and that they weren't crocodile tears, but it was confusing to feel what she did, love and hatred, both at the same time. She leaned down and kissed Laurie on the cheek, only for the sake of appearances.

She collected a chair from the other side of the room and positioned it next to Sara who was already talking non-stop to her dad.

'This is so great Dad, you look really well, and we can't wait to get you home. Can we Mum?'

'No, we can't.'

Laurie smiled over at Hope. 'I'm looking forward to getting home too,' he said rather hesitantly.

Sara looked from one to the other of her parents smiling and shaking her head. 'You two, you're hardly full of enthusiasm, are you?' And then after a moment, 'I know, this is a big day for all of us. Oh yeah, I just remembered, Mum has a bit of a hangover – that's why she's quiet today!'

Laurie didn't actually say anything but the look of surprise on his face was enough to encourage Sara on.

'Yeah, she hit your whiskey bottle last night, and I found her asleep on the settee this morning. Had to cook her a fry up and everything. She is only just beginning to look normal now!'

'But you don't like whiskey,' said Laurie.

'I know, but you know how these things happen. It starts off with just one and before you know it, well anyway, I won't be doing it again for some time.'

Laurie looked confused and so Sara summed up to clarify for him.

'Actually Dad, she was really upset. There, she must really love you.' It had seemed such an innocent thing to say and yet the awkward silence in the room suggested otherwise, and now it was Sara's turn to feel confused. And so, she returned to the safety of the noise of her chatting.

'We haven't even asked; how are you feeling? You look amazing, not like you've been in an accident or ill or anything.'

Laurie nodded, acknowledging his daughter's comments. 'I don't feel too bad actually, a little sore and bruised but really not too bad.'

'And do you remember anything about the accident?'

Hope, who had been sitting observing the interaction between her husband and daughter, suddenly looked up with more animated interest which didn't go unnoticed by Laurie.

'No,' he said rather vaguely. 'I don't really remember anything.'

I bet you don't, thought Hope, how very convenient.

'Oh, that's a shame.' Sara sounded genuinely disappointed. 'Perhaps your memory will come back in time, as you get better.'

'Yes, hopefully it will. We'll just have to wait and see.' He looked over at his wife who was staring back at him, neither of them able to read the other's thoughts.

'Anyway, lots of people have been phoning and asking after you. They'll be able to come here and visit now although you'll be home soon so I suppose they might as well wait until then. Oh yeah, Mum's going to look into getting a private room for you.'

Sara turned towards Hope for confirmation, but her face was blank.

'That's right isn't it? You said you were looking through the insurance policy.'

'Yes, that's right,' said Hope an almost menacing tone to her voice as she continued to hold Laurie's stare, neither of them even daring to blink. Sara continued to talk non-stop, mostly about nothing in particular. There was no mention of university or her stay with Gemma, Hope noted.

Neither she, nor it seemed Laurie, had the energy to join in and eventually Sara, frustrated and unable to decipher the atmosphere in the room and finding that even her constant chit-chat wasn't helping, finally gave up.

Without much ceremony, Hope and Laurie exchanged pleasant enough good-byes. Sara leaned in carefully to give her father a hug, promising they'd be back tomorrow.

Alone and exhausted, Laurie sank back against the pillows, and closed his eyes. He was too tired to think. And yet he had so much thinking to do. He'd just told his wife and daughter that he was looking forward to going home. And it was true, he was. He had to admit, he couldn't wait to be home with his family.

What had he done? He'd made a mess of everything.

Chapter 16

They walked back to the car in silence. Hope knew her head would be spinning at this point. She also knew her daughter had picked up on something in the hospital room that she was struggling to interpret. But silence was for the best at this point. Or at least a change of subject.

'Let's go somewhere for lunch. Do you fancy that?'

'Yeah, that would be great. We can celebrate.'

Hope looked at her quizzically.

'Celebrate that Dad will be home soon.'

'Where would you like to go?'

'It's got to be The Yorkshire Grey. Shall we?'

'No, not there.' Hope could feel her heartbeat quickening, remembering the last time she was there, just a few short days ago.

'Why? It's Dad's pub, the obvious place to go. And they've probably all heard about Dad so we can tell them that he's okay and he'll be coming home soon.'

'No! Not there.' It came out sharper than Hope intended but she was adamant they would not be going to that pub today.

'How about The Flower Bowl? It's a lovely little restaurant. It's always nice in there.'

'Okay then.' Poor Sara, this whole day was becoming one big ball of tangled confusion and weirdness, and she was beginning to lose the will to figure it out.

They got into the car and Hope drove off, both silent with their own thoughts. Hope was relieved Sara didn't push the point of going to the pub.

'I must phone Gran this afternoon and tell her what's happened.'

'You haven't told her yet?'

'You know what she's like Love; she'll worry herself silly. I've had enough to deal with the last couple of days. But today she'll be expecting Josie to visit, and I've got to try to explain that Josie's in Bali and I'm not and your dad's in the hospital.'

Sara puffed out a weary sigh. Hope ignored her.

'Here we are. I remember they do excellent soup here, all home-made too. I think we're going to need something hot; I don't like the look of that sky up there, looks to be full of snow.'

Sara glanced up at the heavy white-grey sky.

'Mm, yeah maybe.' She was obviously still distracted, but then added, 'I hope it's not snowing when Dad comes home. It'll make things really difficult for getting him around.'

'Come on, let's get inside, I'm starving.' The restaurant was busy and no wonder – the immediate warmth inside was perfectly inviting and the smell of freshly baked food; roast chicken, fried onions and fresh bread couldn't have been more welcoming.

Within seconds, they were met by the head waitress. 'Good afternoon ladies. Table for two?'

'Yes please,' said Hope, looking past the waitress into the restaurant and noticing a perfectly placed table. 'Can we have that one over there, the one by the fire, that would be lovely.'

'Yes of course.' The waitress turned and led them to their table. Hope and Sara settled themselves, ordered a pot of tea for two and picked up their menus to look through.

'Well, this is nice, don't you think? Better than some old pub.'

'Yeah, it's lovely here but I just thought it would be good to go and see some of Dad's friends to let them know how he is and everything.'

Hope suddenly realised how frustrating it must be for Sara with all this strange behaviour going on and not understanding what it was all about.

'I know darling, and you're absolutely right, perhaps we should have gone there although I should think we'll be seeing enough of your dad's friends when they all want to visit over the next few weeks – we'll probably have more than enough of them! Anyway, we are here now, and this is very nice isn't it, let's just enjoy it.'

'Yeah okay,' said Sara rather sullenly as she put her head down seemingly studying the menu with great intent.

'Wow, Sara, look at all those delicious cakes!'

Sara looked over towards where her mother was indicating the dessert trolley. It was crammed full of gorgeous gateaux and delicate patisserie, some decorated with pretty pastel icing while others were heavy with thick rich dark chocolate frosting.

Sara turned back to her menu with a barely audible 'Mm.'

Piqued by her daughter's attitude and knowing full well that if her father were here, she would be enjoying herself, Hope was now on a mission.

'Well, I'm going for it.' Hope pointed with her index finger to the very bottom of the menu. 'It says here that you can have a sample plate of six different desserts. That's what I'm going to have.'

Finally, Sara looked up at her mother. 'Aren't you going to have something proper for lunch? I thought you wanted soup,' she said rather disdainfully, almost critically.

Hope shrugged her shoulders, just for the moment enjoying the fact that she was annoying her daughter and although she realised how stupid it was, she carried on regardless.

'I'm still quite full after our breakfast this morning. I really fancy something sweet and sticky. How about you?'

Sara straightened in her chair, and with the faintest of a weary sigh, closed the menu with a definite disapproving look on her face. 'I'll have the vegetarian lasagne.'

'Okay, let's order.'

They spoke little until their food arrived, merely affirming what a nice restaurant it was and how busy it was for a freezing cold Monday afternoon in April.

Hope looked across the table at Sara's very delicious-smelling vegetable lasagne. Having eaten a slice of pear and caramel tart, and half a mini white chocolate and whiskey gateaux, the sugar rush was already hitting her. And the whiskey flavour was beginning to make her feel sick. Perhaps Sara could be tempted after all.

'Would you like to share some of mine? There's plenty here and I don't think I'll be able to eat all of it.'

'No, it's fine. I'll be okay with this. Anyway, you ordered it, you eat it.' There may have been a hint of nasty pleasure in her comment, but Hope couldn't be sure. The sly smile on her daughter's face did nothing to help her decide. She put down her fork and drank some tea, deciding defiantly that she would eat every single cake and crumb on her plate. And anyway, they could both play sly games.

'So, how's university going?'

Sara closed her eyes very briefly but otherwise gave nothing away. 'Oh Mum, you always ask. And it's just the same, it's always the same. Everything's fine.'

'Well, just tell me, you know, what you get up to. How your studies are going. You never really tell me anything, I'd just like to know, that's all. I'm interested, like any mother would be.'

At that point the waitress appeared at their table. 'Everything OK ladies?'

'Yes, thank you,' they answered in unison.

'Can I get you another pot of tea?' she asked, figuring it would take Hope some considerable time to eat her way through the remaining cakes on her plate.

'Yes please, that would be lovely,' agreed Hope.

Sara was concentrating on scooping up the last gooey remnants of her lasagne. The moment was gone, the topic of university most definitely closed. But Hope wasn't giving up just yet.

'And so, how's Gemma these days? Did you have a nice evening together?'

'Yeah, it was fine,' said Sara with her mouth full, scraping the plate for food that wasn't there, refusing to look at her mother.

She can't lie while looking me in the eye, Hope noted for the second time in as many days, and she couldn't decide whether this merited as a plus or not.

'How is her grandmother? Wasn't she very ill a while ago? I remember you saying how close they are as a family. And wasn't she about to move in with them? She wasn't really able to look after herself anymore, and rather than go into a home, she was going to live with them. I'm sure that's what you told me.'

Sara busied herself, placing her dish and cutlery neatly to the side of the table. 'Yeah, I think so.' She looked up, finally meeting her mother's eye. 'What? I don't know, I can't remember. You seem to know more than me.'

She was fussing again, this time pouring the last of the tea into her cup and in her flustered state, clipped the teaspoon sending it clattering noisily to the floor. As she bent over to pick it up, Hope watched, aware that she had her daughter rattled, but didn't feel any sense of satisfaction. Instead, she felt guilty. Who knew what was going on in her daughter's life? Sadly, she didn't, and until Sara was ready to confide, perhaps she should leave well alone.

Sara glanced around the restaurant, at anyone or any direction other than at her mother. Her face was flushed red, partly from the heat of the open fire but not entirely. She almost looked like she was about to cry, and a sudden rush of sympathy and love washed over Hope. Their tea arrived and Hope poured for them both.

'Let's drink this then how about we go along to King's Bookshop for a good long browse? I haven't been there in ages.' Then as an afterthought, she added, 'I see your dad's favourite author has a new release. You could pick that up for him. It'll make his day.'

Sara was nodding her head gently in agreement, finally lifting her eyes to meet her mother's, smiling softly.

In the King's Bookshop, Hope had a good look around the cookery book section, as she always did whenever she had the opportunity of browsing around a real bookshop.

And as ever, she couldn't help but feel a sense of relief to see that there wasn't anything on the shelves to seriously rival her work in the niche market of children's cookery books.

Sara predictably made an immediate beeline for the Crime Fiction section, searching for her dad's all-time favourite author and his latest release.

Clutching a hardback copy, Sara met up with her mother where she knew she would be by now – in the spiritual health section. Not that this was an interest they shared. She already had three books in her arms; one on meditation - she'd dabbled for years but wanted to practice something more advanced. Sara rolled her eyes to the ceiling when she saw the second book, on Angels. And the last book on top was entitled 'Gratitude, For All Things'. Sara had no idea what that was all about. Hope had chosen it on impulse and felt the irony of it now as she noticed Sara's disparaging look.

Sara hugged her father's gift to her chest, turning away as she muttered, 'I don't know why you're buying all those; you won't have much time for reading when Dad comes home.'

Hope actually narrowed her eyes with distaste as her daughter walked away to the counter to pay. With her arms full of books, she felt a sudden impulse to lob them, one at a time, at the back of her daughter's head.

Suddenly shocked at herself, she stood stock still on the spot and closed her eyes. What on earth was she thinking? What sort of a mother was she to think such things? It felt like her life was collapsing around her like the proverbial house of cards – flimsy and fragile with no foundation, no substance. And she didn't know how to save it, how to stop it from falling.

Hope opened her eyes to see a very young boy staring up at her, wide eyed as if she were a character out of Harry Potter.

'Were you sleeping? he asked. 'Standing up?'

Hope smiled. 'No, I was, well, I was just resting'. The little boy ran off. Hope sighed; had she sank so low as to be scaring young children now?

Over at the counter Hope paid for her books. Sara was waiting for her by the door.

'Didn't you get anything for dad?' The condescending look on her daughter's face was just about too much. Hope inhaled to reply, whether with an equally blunt comment or something more deserving, she never got to find out.

As they opened the door to exit the shop, a young woman came dashing through. Gemma. Hope noted the range of looks on Sara's face, starting with surprise turning to shock then a rapid dawning on her of how unholy inconvenient this was.

Gemma was quickly followed by a couple of girlfriends but swung around.

'Hi Sara. How are you?' She reached out to touch Sara's arm. 'I'm so sorry I haven't been in touch. Thanks for the birthday card. And I would love to meet up, but my gran died a few weeks ago, her funeral was just last week, and my mum is all over the place.'

Gemma glanced back to where her friends were hovering, waiting for her.

'I'd better go. I'll text you; we'll make a date. For definite.'

'Yeah, OK, great.'

Gemma disappeared on her way and Sara caught her mother's eye for a split second before diverting her gaze immediately to the ground, looking for all the world like a naughty, caught-out five-year-old.

Hope seized the moment and responded in kind. 'Home, for you, young lady.'

Chapter 17

Hope parked on the drive and was hardly surprised to see Sara quickly escape out the car, her keys at the ready to unlock the front door before she disappeared upstairs.

She, by contrast, took her time, wearily and mechanically releasing the seat belt before reaching behind her for her handbag, getting out and locking the car. She knew Sara would be out of sight in her bedroom and that she probably wouldn't come out for some time.

She needed to decide how to play this. She could march in, slam the door, scream at her daughter to come down and explain herself this very minute, but as much as the impulse was there, this wasn't her style and anyway she knew it wouldn't achieve what she really wanted – for her daughter to talk to her and explain what was going on in her life.

Why was she still cashing maintenance cheques even though she was no longer attending university? Why was she lying about meeting up with Gemma? And whoever she was meeting up with – why did they have to be such a big secret?

The house was cold, and Hope switched on the heating. She looked inside the fridge, still not feeling great after her sugar-laden lunch and took out a tub of hummus which she ate with half a bag of tortillas, relishing the savoury snack.

She realised she hadn't eaten a proper meal for days and resolved to prepare a good dinner that evening. Perhaps she could entice Sara out of her room to really talk to her.

With a cup of tea and tucked up on the sofa, she pulled a throw over her legs and balanced a cookery book on her knees just as Lulu decided to jump up and totally obscure her view.

'Do you mind? I'm trying to find something to cook.' The kitten continued to thread its way over Hope's arm, standing on the book then sliding off which caused Hope to lose her grip. The book fell heavily to the floor and Hope leaned over to retrieve it which was particularly awkward as Lulu decided she was staying exactly where she was in the middle of Hope's lap.

She grabbed the book with one hand and carefully lifted it back on to the sofa, its heavy glossy pages falling open at a particular recipe. Hope stared and grimaced. She'd cooked this dish numerous times over the years – Lancashire Hotpot. It was Laurie's all-time favourite meal.

Hope stared at the picture. Over the years, she'd tweaked the recipe, little by little, until she'd perfected it to hers and Laurie's taste. Would she ever cook it again for him – and with the same love and care?

She flipped over the page to a recipe she'd never tried before. It was for Cock-a-Leekie Pie, not something she would normally be tempted to try but at this moment, something different, seemed like a good idea. A quick scan down the list of ingredients confirmed she had everything in stock. Preparing and cooking a good meal that evening would provide the perfect occupation of her time and more important would provide the perfect distraction for her overthinking mind.

From the outset, Hope broke her own golden rule – she wasn't organised. In no time at all, she was surrounded by too many mixing bowls and utensils; weighing out ingredients she needed now while vegetables that should have been lightly sautéed were burning in the frying pan.

Her pastry was too soggy, sticking in a sticky mess to the worktop, and her hands covered in goo. She was seriously tempted to throw the lot in the bin. There were pizzas in the freezer.

Suddenly, a door slammed above, and Sara stomped down the stairs.

Hope threw more flour onto the squidgy mess of dough, trying to form it into a mound of something she could actually roll out.

Sara burst into the kitchen and without even acknowledging her mother, she slammed an empty mug onto the draining board before yanking open the fridge door, peering inside but not finding anything to tempt her. She sighed noisily and slammed it shut again.

The noise was invasive and rattled Hope's nerves; Sara was irritatingly and obviously demanding attention. Hope snapped.

'What are you banging around for? It's me who should be angry.'

Sara snorted. 'You're always angry.' She immediately looked sheepish, knowing that what she'd just said was completely untrue. Hope stared at her with exactly the same thought in mind but knew it was a waste of time to expect an apology.

'Actually Sara, you're the one who's always angry. Do you want to tell me why?' She shook the surplus flour from her hands and wearily went over to the sink to wash the sticky mess off. She sighed quietly, looking over at the mess of her kitchen and wishing she hadn't started. Sara stood there in silence - Hope had expected her to storm off. Drying her hands, she looked expectantly into her daughter's face, but it was blank. It looked as though all the fight had finally gone out of her but there would be no heart to heart today.

'Do you fancy pizza for dinner?'

Sara looked at the unusual mess of her mother's kitchen and smiled sympathetically, nodding in agreement as she began to help with the cleaning up.

They worked together in silence. Sara scraped the remains of the dough goo from the worktop and used lots of hot water to wipe it clean. Hope took two pizzas from the freezer and put them in the oven, laying the table with plates and cutlery.

'Shall we have wine?' Sara asked, taking a bottle of red from the rack and studying the label.

'Yes, good idea.'

Hope watched as her daughter replaced the bottle and took another, surprised that she appeared to understand the abundance of information on the label.

'This one looks good. Malbec, should be good.' Sara nodded her head, acknowledging that she had made a good choice.

Hope took the pizzas from the oven and placed them on trivets on the kitchen table. Sara began cutting a slice even before they'd sat down.

'It'll be hot! You'll burn your mouth.'

Sara gave her mother a look, reminding her that she was no longer five years old and knew that cheesy pizzas coming out of the oven would be extremely hot. But she was smiling, and then they were both laughing as she took a bite, unable to eat it, sucking in air to cool her burning mouth. They sat down opposite each other, sharing pizzas and drinking wine.

It was a very pleasant meal. They were both relaxed and easy company for each other, both distracted from their respective troubles and worries. Maybe it was this unfamiliar feeling of contentment, the warmth of comfort food, and a little too much wine mixed with the sheer exhaustion of the last few days that caused Hope to not so much burst the bubble, as completely shatter it.

Holding her glass of wine in hand, she looked across at her pretty daughter.

'I know you're not at university anymore.' She was shocked at herself for actually saying the words out loud. But she managed to keep her cool and held her daughter's stare as she lifted her eyes to meet her mother's. Sara swallowed hard. Hope waited.

Sara looked down at the few pieces of leftover cold pizza. 'Who told you?'

'Why have you left?' Neither answered the other's question. 'Why have you left?' Hope repeated, driving home the message that she would have her question answered before giving any information herself. 'Well?'

Sara fidgeted, and took a deep breath, struggling to find suitable words. Without looking up, she finally answered. 'I'm with someone,' she said almost defiantly.

Hope waited for the necessary explanation to follow, getting frustrated now at having to eke out every scrap of information. 'You have a boyfriend. And? That doesn't explain why you've left university.'

'We're together. We're living together.'

'For goodness' sake Sara, that isn't a reason to give up your education.'

'I don't know what the big deal is; you were married at my age.'

'I was grown up at your age!' Hope sighed. This wasn't what she wanted, and she took some deep breaths to calm herself. 'So, you're with someone, that hardly needs to be a secret, does it?'

Sara got up and began collecting the dinner things from the table. And now Hope was pacing the kitchen, irritation raging through her. And then a thought dawned on her. 'Does it need to be a secret?'

Sara was rinsing the plates in the sink before placing them in the dishwasher but even turned away from her mother, Hope could detect the discomfort she was causing.

'Sara. Who is he?' Sara turned to face her mother.

'He's someone I met at Uni. We've been together quite a while.'

'He's one of your lecturers, isn't he?'

'A professor actually.' She was unable to stop herself.

'I hope that wasn't supposed to impress me.'

'You don't know anything about him. You can't judge.'

'I can judge that he's a good few years older than you, and he should never have let you leave university, after the way you worked to get in there.'

'I'm going to find somewhere else and continue my studies. He's going to help me find somewhere.'

Hope laughed. 'Which means he hasn't yet, in over a year, and he obviously didn't discourage you from leaving in the first place.'

Sara was losing some of her fight. She attempted to close the argument. 'Anyway, it's not really anything to do with you.' But Hope's anger was in full force now, and after all this time, she wasn't holding back.

'Isn't it? And the tuition fees that I've paid and the monthly allowance cheques – are they nothing to do with me?'

'That's just typical. It always has to come down to money.'

'No, it doesn't come down to just the money. It comes down to being honest and not having to put up with all the deception that we've had to for all this time.'

The word 'we' caught Sara's attention. 'Does Dad know?'

The question answered Hope's own question that had been rattling around in her brain for some time. 'No, he doesn't. But he will.'

'And anyway, I didn't spend the money.'

Hope was already walking out of the kitchen as Sara spoke, leaving those last few words ringing in her ears. She went through to the living room, not knowing what to do with herself when she got there. The crystal whiskey decanter glinted and caught her eye but as tempting as it was, she would not be driven to drinking away her problems.

She went upstairs to her bedroom and sat on the edge of the bed, leaning forwards, elbows on knees, her head in her hands. The room, her most personal space, didn't provide the sort of peace she needed. A jumper of Laurie's was slung over the back of the chair, his current novel with a bookmark in place on the bedside cabinet. And his side of the bed, empty without him in it for the last few nights.

She rubbed her face with her hands, weary beyond measure after the events of the day although she felt some relief in that Sara hadn't actually spent her university money. It was a small but significant symbol of integrity by her daughter. But other than that, what had she got herself into?

Hope ran herself a bath in the en-suite, adding calming aromatherapy oils of neroli and chamomile. She soaked herself for a good half hour, planning an early night of reading with a mug of hot milk and honey.

Down in the kitchen, Sara had tidied the dinner things away and cleaned to perfection. All the lights downstairs had been switched off except for a few worktop lights. The room looked warm and cosy, inviting, homely. She heated some milk, flicked off the lights, locked the front door and went up to bed.

Having read the same paragraph over at least three times without remembering a single word, Hope rested the book on her lap and sipped her hot milk. She heard a light tap on her bedroom door and was surprised to see Sara's head peek inside.

'Mum?'

'Yes, Love?'

''It's true what I said, I haven't spent your money. It's in a separate bank account to give back to you at some point.'

'OK, Love. We can talk about it another time. Thank-you for letting me know though.' Hope smiled, friendly but cautiously, not too expectantly. She didn't want Sara to leave and had to be careful with what she said. 'What's his name?'

'Sam.'

'Sam, that's nice. Is he very much older than you?'

'He's thirty-nine. It's not so very old.'

'No, it's not,' said Hope baulking at the thought that he was actually only a few years younger than her. There was a pause of a few seconds, both treading carefully, trying not to allow this fragile bubble of niceness to burst.

'How did you find out that I'd left?' Sara just managed to keep her tone of voice even, not to let the question betray her suspicion that she was being watched by her mother.

Hope smiled. 'It seems you're a victim of your own mother's success as a famous author.'

Sara looked at her mother, confused. She knew Hope hated any reference to her being famous or becoming a celebrity cook.

'It's down to one of your housemates, Audrey? Audrey Redfern wasn't that her name?'

Sara nodded, not sure where this was going.

'I distinctly remember her name; it sounds like Audrey Hepburn the actress. And also, Audrey is quite an unusual name for a girl your age. Anyway, she must have found out that I was your mother, or maybe you told her about me. She has two much younger sisters who like my books, is that right?'

'Yeah, that's right. Audrey told me they were crazy about your books and they had just started collecting the special kiddie's equipment.'

'Well, her mum emailed me and excused herself for being cheeky, but could I send a couple of books and sign them for the girls. Obviously, I agreed, scribbled a note down on a scrap of paper and promptly forgot about it for a few weeks. I felt so bad when I found it that I put a package together of books and some goodies from the shop. I didn't want your friend bad-mouthing me to you!' Hope laughed.

Sara smiled, uncomfortably aware of the irony to come.

'Anyway, Audrey's mum phoned to thank me and of course we got chatting. And then she mentioned what a shame it was that you'd left university especially as you had been doing so well with your studies and in exams too.'

Sara shuffled on the spot. 'What did you say?'

'Very little. What could I say? I was embarrassed that she knew more about my daughter than I did. Oh, I don't know, I mumbled something about it not being a good time for you.'

Sara stared across the room, nodding her head as if to acknowledge the awkwardness her mother must have felt during that conversation. 'I'm sorry.'

Hope let the sound of the apology linger on the air for a while. She reckoned this had earned her a few more probing questions.

She cocked her head to one side, hoping to lessen the directness of her question, choosing her words carefully. 'So, your Sam, has he been married?'

Sara nodded her head. 'But they've been separated for a while.'

Hope smiled sympathetically. 'And, does he have children?'

Sara looked at the floor and sighed, finally nodding confirmation. 'Mum, don't.'

'OK, OK, I won't ask any more. As long as he's looking after you.'

'I have a job.' She spoke too soon, the defensiveness apparent again in her voice and now she would have to explain. 'It's only shop work, just for now, so that I can contribute.'

'Yes, of course. That's good.'

'I'm going to bed now. Night Mum.'

'Good night Love. Sleep well.'

Hope abandoned her book and her drink, clicked off the bedside lamp and lay there in the darkness knowing she would never be able to sleep tonight with her world of worries, all competing for attention in her mind.

Chapter 18

Josie finished eating her breakfast, looked around her and tried to take in the amazing setting. She was on the other side of the world, on the edge of a lush tropical forest, drinking a cup of tea.

The table had been laid with a variety of food to suit every taste and she'd dabbled with a little of everything; croissants; scrambled eggs and bacon; Danish pastries, and lots of fruit. There were strawberries and bananas and a platter of melon slices in a range of pretty colours from pale yellow, soft green, peach, orange through to the deepest pink.

She'd never eaten fruit for breakfast before and she couldn't imagine what Ross would say if she ever served it to him on a Sunday morning instead of the traditional full English fry-up. But it was delicious, and she had to stop herself from eating. She'd heard of Delhi-Belly; too much tropical fruit could land her with a Bali-Belly.

There was so much food left over, she wondered what she was supposed to do with it. She couldn't possibly have eaten it all but if it was left outside, it would be ruined in the heat.

She got up and walked to the edge of what appeared to be her own private garden, looking out across the resort to see if there was anyone waiting to take the food back, but there was no-one around. It was as if she had the whole place to herself.

She sighed, a little confused; there was nothing else for it – she would have to take it inside and store it in the little kitchen area. She'd noticed earlier that there was a small fridge in there.

As she traipsed back and forth, her mind turned to the appointment Hope had made with the retreat specialist. She really didn't want to go but decided it would be rude not to turn up and anyway, she would simply explain that she was only staying for one week and therefore wouldn't be needing any health plan – she'd be finished with the specialist in about five minutes.

Josie strolled through the lush gardens, so quiet except for the call of birds and the breeze gently rustling the dense vegetation of the forest just beyond. She looked up at the trees, and then further up at the intense blue sky. The colours were amazing; the grass bright green, and throughout the garden, masses of vibrant red and yellow, orange and pink huge tropical flowers, as if everything had just been freshly painted.

There was also something different about the light here; it was as if her focus had been slighted adjusted to make everything that little bit sharper, clearer. She kept stopping to study a particular flower or follow the call of a bird but had to remind herself she was supposed to be somewhere by now and hurried herself on.

In the lounge area of the main retreat building, she was welcomed by Katherine, the retreat health specialist, and already they'd been talking for over fifteen minutes. Katherine had listened with compassion as Josie explained why Hope hadn't been able to come and how she'd been persuaded to take her place.

'This isn't really my kind of holiday; all the yoga and meditation and everything.' She laughed nervously, realising perhaps this wasn't the most tactical thing to be saying.

'What sort of things do you like to do? How do you relax at home?'

Josie paused, uncomfortably aware that she was struggling for an answer to what was really a very simple question.

'Well, I'm married to Ross,' she said, as if that explained everything.

Katherine smiled and nodded encouragingly.

'That keeps me busy enough; looking after him and the house.' She stopped talking, again aware that this was not the sort of answer Katherine was after. She didn't have any hobbies – it was an awkward realisation.

Most of her time was taken up with looking after the house and running around after Ross. And although she felt anxious and stressed a lot of the time, she didn't actually take any steps to de-stress herself at the end of each day – apart from a few glasses of wine which probably didn't count as a healthy answer on a wellbeing retreat.

'And anyway, although Hope booked her holiday here for six weeks, I won't be able to stay that long. I'm only staying for one week.'

Katherine smiled serenely. 'Oh, I'm sure you'll stay longer than that,' she said nodding at Josie with such certainty as if she were looking into a crystal ball. She was flicking through some leaflets and handed them over together with a glossy brochure.

'Your friend, Hope, booked herself on our most luxurious wellbeing retreat package. Every activity that's described here, has already been paid for. You can choose any activity or treatment as many times as you like; yoga classes, meditation groups and nature walks.'

She looked across at Josie's blank face and tried again.

'Or there are various massage therapies you could try, a range of beauty treatments and facials.'

Josie's expression had now changed to one of slight interest, and Katherine quickly scooped up a couple more leaflets and handed them to her.

After a while they concluded their meeting and walked outside to the garden.

'I hope you enjoy your stay here in Bali. If there's anything you'd like to discuss, just ask at reception for me.'

'I'm sure I will and thank-you for all this information and everything. It'll definitely keep me busy for the week.'

'You're very welcome. And, if I were a gambling person, I would take a bet that you will stay for longer than one week.' Katherine smiled her beautiful, serene smile before walking away in the opposite direction.

Deep in thought, Josie walked towards the pool, sunk into the lush grass, aiming for one of the loungers dotted around. Day One, and despite there being so much on offer, she didn't know what she was going to do with herself for the rest of the day.

She barely noticed a couple sitting side by side on a sun lounger until they called out in a distinctly American accent.

'Hi there.' A well-groomed man in his early sixties smiled up at her.

'Hello.'

'How you doing? You look a little lost, if you don't mind me saying.'

Josie smiled back, and then at who she presumed to be his wife. 'Yes, actually, I am a bit.'

'This your first time in Bali?'

'Yes.' And it'll probably be my last, was what she was thinking.

'This is our twelfth time.'

'Really?' Josie couldn't keep the shock from her voice.

He laughed, holding out his hand. 'Yes, really. I'm Bob by the way, and this is my wife Mary. Take a seat here, join us.'

Josie shook hands with Bob and Mary and sat down on the lounger opposite them.

'Wow, twelve times.' She wasn't quite sure how to ask the question. 'What is it, that keeps you coming back?'

Mary answered, with a gentle, confident voice. 'From the moment we step off the plane, we feel ourselves let go, relax and decompress. Life here is simple and everything moves at a slower pace. This time we're here for a Soul Adventure and we know when we leave, it'll be with a renewed sense of purpose and optimism.'

Josie nodded, slightly awestruck. 'How long are you here for?'

'We've been here a week already, and we're heading home in four weeks. Back to Florida. How about you?'

'Oh, I'm only here for one week. I could stay for six if I wanted to, but I'm going home in a week.'

Bob and Mary looked at each other and smiled a knowing smile then they both looked back directly at Josie.

'For sure, you'll be here a lot longer than that.'

Chapter 19

'Mum. It's Martha on the phone for you.'

Hope came into the kitchen from the garden and Sara handed over the phone, pulling a face and making Hope smile. Martha could be a little full-on sometimes.

'Hi Martha. How's everything?'

'Oh, all fine, yes everything's fine. I was just calling to see how Laurie was.'

'He's OK. Yes, we're expecting him to be allowed home possibly next week.' Hope dredged her reserve for a show of enthusiasm. 'We're getting everything ready for him here, and of course really looking forward to him being home.'

'That's great. And you still have Sara there?'

'Yes, she's here at the moment but actually she's heading back to her place tonight for a few days and then she'll be back again when Laurie's here.'

Hope's mind wandered back to earlier that morning. While she and Sara were having breakfast, Sara told her she would be heading back to Sam's place again for a few days.

She would worry about her. It didn't help that she now knew where she was and who she was with; knowing the facts simply gave her something concrete to worry about.

'Oh that's good.' Martha sounded distant and distracted, as though she were deep in thought. 'And you visit him every day I suppose?'

'Yes, I think it would look a little odd if I didn't show my face at least once a day.' Hope cringed at her own words; she'd been a little too honest there. It was as much as she could do to visit the hospital at all. It was much easier with Sara there as she could leave her to do most of the talking, but it would be difficult over the next few days when she was back in Leicester.

'Anyway, he's fine, sitting up in bed, doing the crossword. I go along some time in the morning and take him fresh supplies or whatever he needs.'

'Has he said anymore? About the accident I mean. Does he remember anything?'

'No, nothing much at all. He has flashes of what he thinks he remembers but he can't be sure.'

'Oh, right. And you visit him in the mornings?'

'Yes, we've just got into that routine. And he's probably a little tired in the afternoon. You know, it'll take a while for him to get his energy back.'

'I suppose it will. Well, I'm glad to hear he's on the mend. It's good news, isn't it? I'll call again in a day or so, if that's alright with you Hope?'

'Yes of course. That's absolutely fine.' Hope hung up, smiling to herself. Martha could be a little overbearing sometimes, but she was a good sort. It was sweet of her to be so concerned for Laurie.

Hope went into the dining room, a good-sized room across the hallway off the back of the kitchen. It was traditionally set with a large oval table and six velvet covered chairs, but it was rarely used anymore.

When Sara was young, her birthday parties had been held in there with a traditional birthday tea and elaborate cake. And afterwards Hope would encourage the children to spill out directly into the garden through the French doors to play games and to work off their overdose of sugar.

They used to have Sunday lunch in there every week and of course Christmas dinner. She stood looking at the tired-looking room trying to remember the last time they'd had a special meal in there all together.

Laurie had wanted to celebrate their wedding anniversary last year. He'd suggested a party, but Hope had laughed that idea out of his mind. He then suggested they invite family and close friends over for dinner but again Hope had shot him down. They were both too busy. She was busy – she remembered they were having some alterations done in the shop and it was all quite chaotic at the time. It seemed sad now that they hadn't done anything to celebrate their special day at the time.

A door slammed upstairs bringing Hope and her thoughts back to the present moment. She got to work and began stacking the chairs over by the French doors ready to take out through the garden into the garage. She then lifted two silver candlesticks off the table and placed them on the dresser. The idea was to empty the room and pack everything away, but she'd forgotten how much stuff there was in there.

Sara appeared in the doorway to see her mother bent overlooking underneath the table.

'Mum, what are you doing?'

Since their very brief heart to heart last night, there'd been a slight clearing of the air and a pleasant easiness over the morning. Hope wasn't allowing herself to be over-optimistic about how long it might last but for the moment, neither of them seemed to the other to be either on the attack or unreasonably defensive. It made life much more pleasant – for the time being anyway.

'I'm trying to figure out how to dismantle this table. Any ideas?'

Sara came further into the room. 'I'll have a look. But why do you want to? Are you clearing this room out? Why now?'

Hope stood and faced her daughter. 'When your dad comes home, he'll have to sleep down here. He won't be able to make the stairs every night and I'm not carrying him up!'

Sara smiled but frowned at the same time. Until just now, she hadn't considered how difficult it would be for her dad to move around the house with his injuries.

'I hadn't even thought of that.' It would be odd to think of him not being upstairs with her mum in their bedroom together.

For Hope, this side-effect of his injuries was a blessing. While it felt very strange being alone in their king-size double bed, she had no idea how she would feel having him sleeping next to her at this point in time. Turning the dining room into a makeshift bedroom for him was a godsend of an idea.

'Your dad won't be comfortable sleeping on the sofa for any length of time. And this seems like the perfect idea. What do you think?'

Sara looked around at the tired-looking room. 'It's a brilliant idea but it hasn't been decorated in here for years. It looks really old fashioned now.'

'You're right it does. But Dad won't be bothered about that. We can make it nice for him; order a new bed, perhaps a bookcase and put some lamps around and perhaps he'll be able to draw in bed. He probably won't want to come out!'

Sara laughed, liking the idea of making it special for his home coming.

'Actually, this is pretty perfect.' Sara turned, surveying the space. 'Eventually he'll be able to hobble out to the kitchen and make himself a drink. He's got the shower room at the end of the hall and when the weather gets a bit warmer, he can have the doors open, go out into the garden or whatever.'

'Yes exactly. I'm glad you approve.'

'Yeah, I do. Actually, I was just coming to tell you that I'd be heading off earlier than I thought, like in a minute, but if you want, I can stay a while longer. I can help you with things in here.'

'Thank-you Love, but I can manage. Although, there is one thing you can do - get under that table and work out how it comes apart. Then I can drag it out to the garage. Although maybe I should just get rid of it. If we decide to change it back and use it as a dining room again, we really ought to get something more modern.' Hope's voice trailed off as the thought occurred to her that, as a family, they may never use it as a dining room again. And looking further into the future, this house, their home may never be the same for any of them.

Sara crawled under the table and looked at the fixings, trying to work out how to dismantle it.

Hope appreciated her offer to stay and help but although it was a good idea to have Laurie in a room of his own, the fact was she resented all the work she would have to do and just wanted it organised as quickly as possible.

If Sara stayed to help, she would want everything to be perfect for her dad and it would drive Hope crazy. And she was already worried she wouldn't be able to keep up this performance of pretending to care much longer.

Sara reappeared from under the table. 'I think it's just a matter of a few screws and the legs should come off. That'll make it a little easier to store, won't it? I'll get the screwdriver.'

'Thank-you, that'll be a great help.'

Sara went through to the kitchen calling back as she rummaged in a small drawer. 'Are you sure you'll be alright getting everything into the garage by yourself?'

'Yes, I'll be fine. You get yourself off. You don't want to get caught in any traffic.'

While Hope struggled to accept the situation of her daughter currently living with a much older married man, for the time being, they appeared to have an unspoken agreement of not actually referring to it. This seemed to be working for both of them, but she knew it wouldn't last.

By mid-morning, Hope had taken the table and all the chairs out to the garage and stacked them at the back. She'd taken everything off the dresser and managed to gently manoeuvre it over to the end wall next to the French doors leaving the longer wall free so that a bed could be put there.

She was worn out already but there was still lots to do. Usually, she would be getting ready to head off to the hospital at this time but she wasn't looking forward to visiting Laurie on her own and so she decided to finish what she'd started and go to the hospital that afternoon instead. And it wouldn't hurt for him to learn not to take everything for granted.

Chapter 20

Josie had agreed to meet up with Bob and Mary in the bar before dinner. She was now rifling through the eclectic mix of clothes she'd hastily thrown into her suitcase looking for something suitable. But what was suitable for dinner on a retreat in Bali? She had no idea. She settled for white jeans and a turquoise chiffon shirt, hoping that smart-casual would be acceptable.

The sun was just setting as she strolled through the garden. Soft lighting, cleverly hidden among the trees and shrubs, cast a surreal glow as she followed the path and as she breathed in deeply, she had to admit it was magical.

Bob and Mary were already seated on high stools at the bar and waved her over as soon as they saw her. She was suddenly very grateful for having met two such friendly people who didn't mind her tagging along. She carefully climbed up on the barstool next to Mary.

'Hi Josie, hey you look great. I love the outfit.'

'Oh, thank-you.' Josie sat up a little straighter, pleased with her choice of clothes. She'd already observed Bob and Mary's casual dress code. Mary was wearing a loose, ankle length smock dress in bright orange, a string of dark wooden beads swinging at her neck. Bob looked comfortable in his beige chinos and pale blue shirt.

'What are you having to drink?' he asked.

Josie looked at their champagne cocktail glasses, filled with a mysterious yellow drink and a slice of lime.

'We're having pineapple coconut martinis. You want to try one?'

'They look yummy. Yes please.' Bob ordered another round and Mary pushed a plate of hors d'oeuvres towards her.

'We're just eating a little something here – this is squid with lime aioli. And this rather exotically named Sate Lilit, is fish. But with a hot chilli sauce, so be careful.'

Josie tentatively had a taste and was pleasantly surprised to find she liked squid and the Balinese fish on a stick.

Her thoughts returned to home and Ross. She thought about him all the time; what would he think to see her eating all this unusual food? They didn't do exotic in their house. Good plain English food was his preference.

Josie took out her mobile phone and checked for messages but there still weren't any. She'd sent a few to Ross and tried calling a couple of times but as yet hadn't received a reply. She was just about to send another message describing her squid experience but changed her mind, suddenly slightly irritated at his petty sulking. She put her phone back in her bag resolving not to check it again that evening.

Bob checked his watch and confirmed that they ought to take their places for dinner. Josie followed them out of the bar and across a small decking area to a wooden pavilion, open on all sides to enchanting views of the gardens. Inside there were four large tables, each set for eight people. One table was already full, and a few other spaces had also been taken.

Once again, Josie was relieved to be able to hide under Bob and Mary's wing. Having to dine with lots of people she didn't know was her worst nightmare, and she was quite happy to be guided now by these experienced Bali tourists.

Bob and Mary sat opposite each other at an unoccupied table, and Josie sat next to Mary. The polished wooden tables were simply but beautifully laid with bowls of exotic flowers floating in water, the light from many candles bouncing off like stars.

They each studied the menus as the dining area gradually filled; guests calling out greetings to their new-found friends and instantly chatting about the activities of their day.

'Hi Alex! Come, join us.' Bob called out to a man entering the pavilion on his own. He was tall and slim, dark haired, clean shaven, and immediately headed for their table. Although he was alone, he had a certain confidence about him that Josie noticed and knew she didn't possess but decided in that moment she'd like to. Alex sat down next to Bob.

'Josie, this is Alex. He's from your part of the world, London in England. Alex, this is Josie.'

Alex reached across the table and gently shook her hand. 'Whereabouts in London do you live?' he asked.

'Actually, I don't live in London, not far out though, a little village near Epsom in Surrey.'

'Right, nice part of the world.' He smiled briefly but didn't pursue the conversation with her, turning instead to talk to Bob. Josie wasn't sure whether to take offence or not. She wasn't here to be chatted up, but maybe that was a little too abrupt.

Mary moved in closer to her, cocking her head conspiratorially towards Alex. 'We met Alex last week,' she whispered. 'He's been here for one week and is staying for just a couple more. He and his wife booked this holiday a year ago, something she'd always longed to do. It was to celebrate her thirtieth birthday and their fifth wedding anniversary. They were planning to start a family afterwards and this was to be their last big holiday before then.'

Josie smiled half-heartedly, not wanting to show much interest in this man. Mary continued.

'Well, can you believe it, the most awful thing happened. His poor wife, at first she thought she'd fallen pregnant already, got herself checked out. And, well, long story short, she wasn't pregnant, but she was terribly ill.'

Mary stopped abruptly, sipped her drink as Bob and Alex shared a joke, laughing and looking across the table at the ladies. 'Shall we order?' said Bob, drumming his fingers on the table.

Mary quickly finished her story. 'Anyway, they couldn't do anything for her, and she died just a couple of months ago. And before she died, she made him promise he would still come to Bali and live the experience for her. How about that?'

Josie stared at her, speechless for a moment. 'My god, that's awful,' she whispered.

'I can highly recommend the Banana Wrapped Steamed Snapper with fragrant Coconut Sauce,' announced Bob loudly. Their table had filled up and Bob appeared to be holding court with everyone listening to his advice. 'Although the Chicken and Lychee curry is hard to beat.'

'Banana Snapper for me, that'll be a first,' said Alex smiling directly at Josie. 'How about you? Have you ever had banana and fish on the same plate?'

'No, never,' said Josie astonished at this man's brave and calm dignity.

'Well, are you in?' He smiled encouragingly.

'Definitely. Banana fish for me.'

Later that evening, Josie lay in bed, gazing into the darkness. It had been a wonderful evening. She smiled to herself at the memory of a banana fish dinner and the fact that there weren't any bananas at all. The fish had simply been steamed in banana leaves. And it was delicious.

Alex had left shortly after the meal and she thought about him now and the tragedy he was having to deal with. He'd lost not just his wife but his future family too. He seemed so calm and composed but he must get so angry, she thought, with what life has dealt him.

Her phone beeped next to her on the bedside cabinet. She picked it up and smiled to see a message from Hope, she was just checking in and wanting to know where her photos were.

Josie had sent two more messages to Ross asking him to let her know that everything was OK but there was still nothing from him.

Chapter 21

As Hope parked at the hospital, she could feel a tight knot of anxiety in her stomach. Taking a deep breath, she walked into the hospital entrance, not in any hurry to get where she was going.

As she walked along the corridor, she glanced at the other patients and their accompanying friends and family, wondering what their stories were. She would lay a bet they were quite ordinary compared to hers.

What would she and Laurie talk about, just the two of them today? As always seemed the case lately, she had many more questions than answers. She could get his attention by telling him all about Sara and her boyfriend - the much older married man with children. But this was hardly the time or place for that.

Without Sara present, was this the right time to let him know she'd found the divorce petition in his room? Should she now demand to know what the hell was going on, and did this mean he wanted to be with someone else? And if so, he could damn well go to her now and let her be his carer.

As Hope waited for the lift, she knew she wouldn't address any of these things, not here in the hospital. Certainly, the anger was still there, bubbling furiously just below the surface. And there was the terrible hurt she had to deal with hour by hour. But there was disbelief too. Part of her just couldn't accept it, it was as if those documents in Laurie's desk drawer could all be part of some terrible mistake. She couldn't bear the thought of their marriage being over and losing Laurie for ever.

She pressed the lift button again, several times, and as she waited, she thought of a safe topic of conversation for what she'd already decided would be a short visit. She would tell him all about how she'd been busy rearranging the dining room and making it into a bedroom for him.

The lift still didn't arrive and with an irritated sigh, Hope pushed against the heavy door that led to the stairwell. Up on the second floor and through a set of double doors into the corridor, it took just a few seconds to get her bearings. She could see the nurses' station up ahead at the end of the long corridor, a little way further on from Laurie's room.

She saw a woman come out of his room and head away from her down the corridor. The absence of a uniform meant she wasn't a member of staff but anyway, Hope recognised her immediately. It was Martha. The woman stopped at the nurses' station and spoke with the young nurse attending the desk. They both smiled and laughed a little before the woman walked away.

Within a few seconds, Hope was standing facing the same nurse who smiled, recognising her immediately.

'Hello Mrs Clements, how are you?'

'Hello, I'm fine thank-you.' Hope pointed along the corridor indicating Laurie's previous visitor. 'That woman who just visited my husband?'

The nurse smiled and nodded; not sure what Hope was asking of her. 'Yes, she's visited a couple of times now. Mr Clements' sister.' The nurse looked puzzled. Surely her patient's wife didn't need confirmation of this.

Hope smiled. 'Yes, I thought it was. I just didn't immediately recognise her there for a moment. It's a shame I missed her.'

'She's been in a couple of times, usually about this time if you wanted to catch her another day.'

Hope made her way to Laurie's room. She was deep in thought even as she opened the door and looked across at her husband in his bed. She'd already decided that this was yet another discovery she would keep to herself for now. It would be easy to jump to conclusions but first she needed to know more. And it should be easy enough to find out for definite – if her business partner was having an affair with her husband.

After the visit from his wife, Laurie lay back against his pillows, exhausted. Hope hadn't stayed long. And she hadn't said much while she was there either. Mostly she'd talked about setting their old dining room up as a bedroom for him which made sense. She was good to go to all that trouble for him. She could have left him to sleep on the sofa.

He screwed his eyes tightly shut and felt them watering with shame. And then he opened his eyes, sat up a little straighter and sniffed, taking a deep breath and reassuring himself that everything would be better as soon as he was home again. How he longed to be back in his home with his family where he belonged.

Hope stopped off at the supermarket but had no idea what was in the numerous bags she now brought in from the car. Impatient, she'd dashed around the shop, with no list to guide her and with a rising temper. She grabbed things indiscriminately from the shelves, her mind miles away, unable to focus on whether they needed butter or milk.

She plonked a couple of carrier bags on the worktop and left the rest on the floor, not even stopping to unpack the freezer goods. Right now, there was something much more important she needed to do.

In her writing room, she switched on her laptop. She waited, impatient for it to fire up, and while she waited, she sat down and grabbed a pen and notepad ready. As soon as she could, she opened her business calendar, immediately scanning the dates.

Since going into business with Martha, she kept a record of the days they took off. They had never agreed anything official regarding holiday allowance, but it was something she'd simply got into the habit of doing. One day she intended to check it through, just to ensure neither of them was taking significantly more time out than the other.

But it wasn't the number of days Martha had taken off that interested her now. It was the actual dates. Starting at the beginning of the current year, she scanned through each month, scribbling the dates down on a piece of paper.

In January, Martha had only taken one day off, in the middle of the month. Hope wrote it down and looked up gazing intently out the window, trying to recall the reason that she'd given but nothing came to mind.

In February, she'd taken a couple of Fridays off but again Hope couldn't remember why that was. And in March, she remembered this one, she'd gone away for a long weekend, taking the Friday and Monday as holiday. That was only a few weeks ago, and already Hope had gone cold with the certainty that something else significant had taken place that same weekend.

She closed the laptop down and sat there for a few minutes gazing out the window into the distance. She was aware of the contrast between the soothing silence of the room, and the chaotic noise in her head. All previous urgency seemed to have left her; she was reluctant now to finish the job, acknowledging there wasn't always satisfaction to be gained from being right.

Eventually she left her room and drifted back into the kitchen having forgotten about the shopping that still needed to be put away. Half-heartedly, she plucked a couple of items from the top of a bag and put them in the fridge, but it was no good, she couldn't rest until she knew for sure.

She dashed upstairs, straight into Laurie's workroom. She remembered seeing his Filofax the other day; going through another person's diary was the last thing she'd ever imagined herself doing but at this moment, there was no other option.

Quickly, before she had a chance to feel guilty, she sat at his desk and placed the scrap of paper with the dates on it in front of her. She then unclipped the cover of his Filofax. Various bits of paper were stuffed into the front, but she ignored these and flipped through to the month of January. She looked at the exact date she'd written down – Thursday 21 January – and found the corresponding date in Laurie's diary. He'd written something in his almost illegible scrawl but after all these years Hope could read it easily. She simply stared. It said 'Artists Fair with M.'

Now she remembered. Very clearly, she remembered Laurie telling her, with great enthusiasm, he would be out for the whole day at an annual artist's fair. Hope tried to remember how Laurie had been at the end of the day when he returned home. She closed her eyes, but she couldn't remember anything. And with an uncomfortable feeling, she had to admit she couldn't remember even asking him about the day or, in fact, having shown any interest in it at all.

Once again, she looked at the dates she'd written down and noted the two in February. More slowly now, she flipped through the pages in Laurie's diary. The first date had a question mark in it – he was obviously planning something which wasn't confirmed at this point. Again, Hope looked out the window for inspiration – did something happen last minute in February? She couldn't recall.

The second February date simply had the word 'Lunch' written in with a very artistic flourish of a happy scroll underneath.

Dismally, Hope checked the last dates she'd noted, a Friday and Monday in March when Martha had said she was going away for a long weekend with a friend. She'd asked who the friend was, and Martha had said something vague and dismissive. Hope hadn't thought any more of it at the time, although she had wondered if her friend had a new man in her life – the irony of it all.

In Laurie's diary, he'd scribbled the word 'Seaside' across the weekend which didn't really give anything away. He was clever enough to be very cautious.

His explanation to her had been that he was off for a long weekend on a watercolour painting course, something he'd wanted to do for a while. As this was only a few weeks before her six week jaunt off to Bali, of course she was pleased he was taking a break for himself. She wasn't about to make a fuss, not that she would have anyway.

Hope tried to recall the day that Laurie had left for his weekend break. Again, she closed her eyes and searched her memory. She remembered him gathering together a few clothes from his wardrobe and stacking them on their bed; t-shirts, sweaters, underwear –

ordinary things. She didn't remember him actually packing which meant she certainly hadn't helped him in anyway. She didn't remember him leaving the house or her wishing him a nice time. She'd probably left early for the shop as usual.

Of course, they had spoken while he was away although it was probably mostly texts. She didn't remember anything significant in those calls or texts to worry her in anyway. At that time, she had no reason to worry; she trusted her husband. She didn't even note the odd coincidence that he and Martha were both away at the same time. They'd been playing a dangerous game at that point. And worst of all they'd been plotting and planning together, against her.

Chapter 22

Bob and Mary had gone for a two-day excursion and Josie had spent the time alone. As strange as it seemed, having only met them a couple of days ago, she missed them.

They described with great animation that they were going to Tenganan to see a water palace and then on to a one-thousand-year-old bat cave temple.

Josie didn't like bats or caves and, in that moment, once again doubted the appeal of Bali that had them coming back to it twelve times.

Afterwards they were going on to a village called Ubud which had a market selling locally made handicrafts. She could understand the appeal of this, almost wishing she were going along with them.

Yesterday she'd stayed alone in her villa for the entire day, dipping in and out of her own private pool and sunbathing on the deck, reading magazines. She didn't miss the television or the computer, hardly giving the results of X-Factor or her Watch List on eBay a single thought. She'd contacted the reception office to request her meals be served here on the terrace.

It surprised her to discover how much she enjoyed the peace and quiet and even her own solitude. Leaving her childhood home and six brothers and sisters behind to marry and move in with Ross, meant she'd never really experienced much time on her own. Even when she'd given up working in the supermarket to become a wife and homemaker, her days seemed endlessly filled with chasing the completion of a never ending 'To-Do' list.

Her villa and its garden and pool were a miniature paradise, and she could have happily spent the whole week not venturing out beyond them. But she couldn't possibly confess that to Hope and so today she'd braved it as far as the infinity pool, sunbathed there for a while drinking young green coconut water direct from the coconut.

She was gradually getting her bearings around the place and knew that the spa pavilion was located about a minute away up by the reception building. Finally, she plucked up the courage to go inside, intending to book a treatment for later in the week. But as it turned out, the massage therapist was free all afternoon and before she knew it, Josie was sprawled half naked on a spa bed, covered in warm fluffy towels awaiting a full body massage.

Despite the warmth of the spa room, the soothing smell of vanilla and cedarwood and the relaxing music, her mind was racing with a kaleidoscope of thoughts.

At first she thought of home. She'd only had one text from Ross, not saying very much at all, only letting her know that he was fine, but he didn't ask anything of her holiday. She thought about how much she missed him, and noticed, not for the first time, a knot of anxiety in the pit of her stomach.

She thought of Laurie in hospital and hoped he was making a good recovery. The emails from Hope hadn't said much about him which was odd. In fact, Hope didn't really sound like herself at all. She decided to phone her later that day.

Bob and Mary took over her thoughts next. She imagined them in their bat cave and hoped they were enjoying themselves. Then her thoughts turned to Alex – she hadn't seen him since her first day when they had all had dinner together. She'd like to know that he was alright, but she didn't know which villa he was staying in and now her mind was filled with crazy images of her knocking on the doors of all sixteen villas on the resort looking for him.

The next thing she knew was the massage therapist gently squeezing her shoulder in an attempt to wake her – she'd fallen into a deep sleep. She opened her eyes, not immediately recognising where she was and tried to sit up, slightly embarrassed that she'd fallen asleep. The lovely smiling therapist quickly reassured her that it was fine for her to rest there for as long as she wanted.

Back outside, the air felt soft and cool on her skin and as she didn't feel like going back to her villa right away, she went for a walk around some of the ten acres of retreat gardens.

She strolled along, trailing her hand along the lush foliage on her way, stopping occasionally to study the intricate petal formations of a tropical flower. She smiled to herself; so, this was what it felt like to be truly relaxed. She closed her eyes and lifted her face up towards the warmth of the lowering sun, breathing deeply.

Suddenly, she heard someone calling her name and turned knowing exactly who it was.

'Josie! Hi there, we're back,' called Mary, as she and Bob walked over to meet her.

'Wow, you look good. Have you been catching some rays? You're glowing.'

'Well, yes, a little. And I've just had a massage. It was amazing – I've never felt so relaxed.'

Mary looked at Bob and they smiled knowingly. 'She's getting hooked,' said Mary. And then she linked her arm through Josie's and walked with her up to the reception pavilion. 'You wait until you've done some yoga and meditation, then you'll discover what it feels like to be relaxed.'

Josie grinned. 'Hm, I don't think so.'

They sat down on a huge sofa with heavy wooden carving and covered in bright coloured silk cushions and were immediately attended by a member of staff offering refreshments.

'How was your bat cave?' asked Josie.

'Amazing!' said Mary. 'Truly amazing. We love visiting the temples. Did you know Bali is often referred to as the 'Land of 10,000 Temples? Of course, we'll never be able to do all of those but we're working our way through.'

'I've never even been to one temple. But I don't think it would be my thing anyway.'

'Get away! You'd love it. You didn't think Bali was your kind of holiday, did you? But look at you now; taking massages, getting out into nature.'

Josie nodded in agreement. She was definitely warming to the place.

'When's our next temple excursion, Bob?'

'In a couple of days – Thursday. Pura Taman Ayun – it means beautiful garden. It's a royal temple.'

'Ah yes, I know the one – looks like it's floating on water. Come with us Josie; I promise you; it will be amazing.'

Chapter 23

After a two-hour bus journey into Ubud, they finally arrived at the temple of Pura Taman Ayun, meaning 'Beautiful Garden'. Josie couldn't help but be captivated as they followed the guide around the complex. She'd never seen anything like it before and was particularly fascinated by the way the temple itself was surrounded by a moat which made it look as though it was floating on water.

She hadn't spoken much during the tour, but Bob and Mary could tell they'd done the right thing by encouraging her to come along.

'This is magical. I love the atmosphere here; the whole feel of the place is amazing. I would never have come if it weren't for you. Thank-you for bringing me.'

After that confirmation, they didn't waste any time before quickly whisking her off to the nearby Pura Tanah Lot – another equally impressive temple although the ambience was completely different.

It was noisy here and busy with crowds of visitors and local vendors trying to encourage the tourists to part with their money. Josie made sure she stuck close to Bob and Mary, worried she would get completely lost without them.

The intricate temple was balanced on a rock, far away from the shore, towering above the sea and they could only get to see it at low tide. To Josie it looked like an expensive china ornament, perfect in every detail.

After half a day of culture and religion, Bob decided it was time to lighten things up a little.

'Let's go see the monkeys,' he said with a cheeky grin.

They arrived at The Sacred Monkey Forest Sanctuary where Mary pointed out the sanctuary guidelines for Josie to read before they went in, adding her own commentary.

'Hang on tight to your handbag, keep it close to you. Don't look the monkeys in the eye, they'll take it as aggression and don't panic if one of them jumps on you.'

'Jumps on me? I didn't know they would do that.'

'It's very unlikely to happen. But if it does, just keep calm and they'll soon jump off. Don't look so worried; you'll love them. They're gorgeous.'

They spent some time wandering among the famous macaque monkeys. Apparently, there were over six hundred monkeys on the sanctuary, and it took Josie a while to get used to them frolicking freely all around her.

Mary bought some bananas, and they fed the monkeys, taking it in turns to take photos of each other.

The last stop of the day before heading back to the resort was the Moonlight Café. It was a favourite of Bob and Mary's and Josie was surprised at the modern design of its very sophisticated interior. She was fast discovering the island of Bali to be one of many contrasts.

Bob led the way through the café to the quieter decking area at the back and they settled themselves on low comfortable settees. They ordered non-alcoholic, fruity fresh cocktails and while they waited for them to arrive, looked through their monkey photos – Josie had taken so many but was now deleting all the fuzzy ones from when she was giggling so much.

She looked across at Bob and Mary laughing at their own pictures. She called out to them to smile for the camera, Bob quickly slipped his arm around Mary's shoulders as Josie clicked off a few shots.

Their brightly coloured drinks arrived, and Mary raised her glass.

'Cheers! Here's to you Josie, for being such great company.'

They all chinked their glasses, Josie feeling a little teary and thinking exactly the same about her new friends.

'Ok, Josie, we feel as if we've known you for ever but actually, we know very little about you at all,' said Mary, smiling up at her expectantly.

'Well, there's not much to tell really. I'm married to Ross.'

'Ah yes, tell us about your husband. How long have you been married?'

'For three years.'

'And you don't have children, do you?'

'No. Well, not yet. I hope to, one day. One day soon, I hope.'

'You'll make a lovely mother. Don't leave it too long.'

'Thank-you. Actually, I've been hopeful for the last three years but no luck yet.'

'Get yourself checked out young lady. Don't leave it, time goes too quick.'

Josie paused, sipped some of her drink. 'I've already had some tests done and apparently, there's no reason why I shouldn't be able to get pregnant.'

'So, that's good news. OK, so what about your husband, Ross, he needs to get checked out, right?' Mary looked at Bob next to her who nodded in confirmation.

Josie looked thoughtful. 'I'm not sure he would go through with that sort of thing.'

'Of course he would. He'd do that for you, surely. I mean, if you want to have a family together - and now that he knows you don't have a problem, he needs to know if everything's OK with him, and if not, what can be done to help.'

'I haven't actually told him that I've had the tests. You see, it's difficult; Ross is a very proud man. He'd take it bad if he thought there was something wrong with him. It would have been better if it was me needing help.'

'Oh, he shouldn't think like that. It might be a case of some simple treatment, and everything's sorted.'

Up until now, Bob had been very quiet throughout the conversation.

'He'll do it, if he loves you and if he wants to have kids with you, of course he'll do it.'

Josie smiled gratefully at him, but sitting there with such a happy, loving couple, she couldn't help wondering over the sort of love she had with Ross. And although she tried to deny it, she didn't think Ross would be bothered if they never had children. And she knew for a fact he would never go to the doctors over this.

Mary sipped her drink, feeling sad as she gazed into the distance. The atmosphere had changed on the day, and she attempted to amend that.

'Ok, what day are we today? Thursday. How about on Saturday, we head out to Lovina Beach, a gorgeous place, not too far away from our resort? It'll be something completely different. You've just got to have a day on the beach while you're here.'

'Ah, sorry I go home on Saturday.'

Mary pulled a silly sad face. 'You can't still be serious about that. You've come all this way, for just one week?'

'I did say all along I was only staying for a week.'

'And your poor friend, who's paid for all this, and wanted you to experience it for her – she'll think you're a lightweight! Listen, I'm kidding. It's your decision. If you feel you must get home, then, of course, you must do the right thing. But it's a shame, you seem to be really getting to know yourself.'

'I'm thinking of Ross. He didn't like me coming away in the first place.'

Bob and Mary both gave her a look. A certain look that said it all. And Josie knew not to say anymore.

Back at The Harmony Resort, they returned to their villas to change, agreeing to meet in the bar for dinner.

Josie slipped into a red dress, admiring her reflection in the mirror, and acknowledging how healthy she looked. She stood there studying the image in the mirror. It was as if someone else was looking back at her.

Mary's words came back to her and it was true; she was getting to know herself. She felt different here, particularly in the company of Bob and Mary. Today she had discovered that temples were fascinating, and monkeys were hilarious fun.

But she was also discovering things about her life which by contrast made her feel very uneasy and were also proving to be inescapable. And she knew she needed to face up to them.

Josie walked quickly through the gardens to the bar, she was a little late. She spotted Bob and Mary in their usual spot and smiled as she joined them.

'Here she is. We thought perhaps you weren't coming,' said Mary.

'I'm sorry, I had to make a phone call.'

'We thought we'd worn you out,' said Bob, smiling affectionately.

'Well yes you have actually, but in a good way. I've had the most fantastic day. Thank-you. Both of you.'

'You're very welcome,' they said in unison.

'Oh, and where did you say we're going on Saturday? The Lovina Beach was it?'

Chapter 24

Hope didn't know how she'd managed to get through the week. She continued to visit Laurie every day in hospital but only stayed for the least amount of time she could get away with.

Their chat was miraculously polite enough despite her wanting to scream at him for what he was planning to do. The clinical, sterile hospital environment was the perfect cover for the lack of warmth in their interactions.

She altered her routine, sometimes visiting in the morning and on other days, in the afternoon – she wanted to come face to face with Martha and find out how she would explain away her sneaky visits.

Fortunately, she'd managed to maintain minimal contact with Martha too. Even though she wasn't thousands of miles away on her dream retreat, she'd left Martha to look after the shop as agreed. One way or another, she reckoned she'd earned some time off, although the last week had hardly been a holiday.

The thoughts in her mind were still whirling around like a merry-go-round. She would wake one morning, angry and defiant, determined that she would not take Laurie back into the house. It could come back until he was better, but that's all.

But as the day wore on, so many happy memories would seep back under her skin. She would think about Sara and how she adored her dad. She didn't think she would cope with her parents separating on top of everything else she had going on.

She might like to play the independent adult but they both knew she was on very shaky ground.

Apart from her daily visit to the hospital, time simply passed by, and she had difficulty justifying what she'd done with herself all day. With no immediately pressing work to get on with and all the household chores up to date, there was nothing that needed her attention.

She made some filter coffee; something she hadn't done for ages, always telling herself she didn't have the time to fiddle about, instant was much quicker. But already the warm coffee aroma had her wishing she'd made the effort more often.

She smirked at the irony of it all; she'd been looking forward to some quality time to herself to think and relax. And here she was being tortured by her thoughts and so unrelaxed she couldn't even sit still long enough to read a book.

She stood at the kitchen counter watching the coffee drip, drip, slowly into the mug. She almost wished Sara were there. Would an argument with her daughter be better than this interminable silence in the house?

Hope poured cream into her coffee and added extra sugar then took it through to the living room. She re-read Josie's last email on her phone and smiled as she read about her visits to some temples and the monkey sanctuary. She'd been surprised when she'd first read that Josie intended staying in Bali for another week. Surprised, but very pleased too.

She flicked on the television and the first programme to appear was Sunday Politics, reminding her that there would be nothing worth watching at this time of the day. And she was too consumed with her own problems to care much about what was going on in the rest of the world.

Even though a Sunday in hospital was pretty much like any other day, she'd told Laurie she wouldn't visit today, telling him she planned to spend the day with her mother. It was an enormous relief not to have to face him as she found it exhausting work continuing the charade between them. She could have confronted him at any time about the papers in his workroom, the visits from Martha, but this wasn't the right time or place and not the way to go about things.

Laurie would be coming home at the end of the week and they would have plenty of time to discuss things in private.

And somewhere deep in the depths of her heart, she was clinging to a tiny hope that just maybe it was all some silly mistake, and they could all continue as they used to be. Although, an increasingly uncomfortable feeling was telling her that the way things used to be was a big part of the problem.

Chapter 25

Having checked several times with Bob and Mary that they really didn't mind her tagging along with them and having been reassured several times that they enjoyed her company, Josie finally relaxed and thoroughly enjoyed their days out and the various excursions that Mary organised.

Each morning, she would have breakfast alone on the terrace overlooking her private pool, and instead of feeling guilty or berating herself for not being brave enough to socialise, she accepted the right to choose what she wanted and relished the peaceful start to her day.

She'd also developed a routine of going for a walk around the gardens each morning. Partly this was to give Bob and Mary at least some of the day to themselves, but it was also in recognition of her need to have some time to herself. Something she hadn't been aware of before now. She was getting to know the grounds of The Harmony Retreat very well and tried to discover something new each day.

Wearing black plimsolls and bright pink shorts, a black t-shirt and a yellow scarf in her hair, she checked in the mirror and decided she looked like a liquorice allsort! She smiled and nodded at her reflection, admitting she looked slightly crazy but that she didn't care.

Today, she was heading out of the gardens, towards the edge of the resort and deeper into the forest. Within minutes, she was walking alongside a tranquil river, towering trees all around and the sound of a waterfall in the distance. She was still within the resort boundaries and felt perfectly safe as she strolled along the manicured pathways, every now and then coming to a resting place with strategically placed lounge beds overlooking a particularly pretty view of the river.

She walked on, intending to stop a while at the next rest place. She could see the river twisting away in the distance and instead of following alongside, she decided to take a short cut through the trees and had only gone a short distance when she saw someone sitting on the trunk of an uprooted tree. She stopped walking, stood completely still.

He had head in his hands and everything about his posture revealed his total distress. Even though he had his back to her, in the muted silence of the forest enclosure, she knew he would hear if she tried to retrace her steps.

She walked on slowly, deliberately making herself heard therefore giving him the chance to get up and walk away if he chose, but he stayed where he was. She gave him a wide berth, by walking out of the forest and back along the river towards him so that he could see her, rather than coming up behind him.

'Hello Alex.'

Finally, he looked up; his weary face unsurprised, as if he knew it was her all the time, but he said nothing.

'I don't want to interrupt you. I'll go if you like. Would you rather I went?'

Alex continued to stare at the ground, but he indicated the space next to him, which she took to be an invite to sit down. They sat together in the quietness for several minutes. Josie was aware that in a previous life, before Bali, she would have chattered non-stop to fill the silence, and yet she was perfectly comfortable with it now.

'We haven't seen you at dinner. I think your friends were starting to worry about you.'

'Bob and Mary?'

'Yes.'

'They're a great couple. Weren't you only staying for one week?'

'I was. And then I met Bob and Mary.'

Alex turned his head to look at her, smiling and nodding.

'Mary told me about your wife. I'm so sorry.'

Alex closed his eyes. His shoulders shook a little. Tears trickled slowly down his cheeks.

Instinctively, she moved along the tree trunk just a little closer and placed her hand on his back, rubbing slowly, squeezing his shoulder. She gazed out over the river and eventually he rubbed his hands over his face and through his hair and sat up a little straighter. Josie let her hand fall to her side.

'Has it helped you, to come out here to Bali?'

'I'm not sure. It's so difficult to be here and see all the things she wanted to do and see.'

'But she wanted you to come?'

Alex nodded. 'Yeah, she did. She insisted, made me promise. And I had to keep that promise.'

'So, you've done what she wanted.'

'Not really. I've been hiding away in my villa. I think the idea was for me to get out there and experience it.'

'Well, I can highly recommend the monkeys.'

He smiled. 'Oh yeah, she was always going on about the monkey sanctuary.'

'Listen, I know it's a bit of a cliché that things happen for a reason and I'm not suggesting that there's a good reason behind anyone losing someone they love. But, take me, for instance; I wasn't supposed to be here. A good friend of mine, as your wife did for you, she insisted that I come. This was supposed to be her holiday, something she'd planned for months. But her husband had a terrible car accident the day before and I'm here taking her place.

'I have to laugh; I used to be a Costa del Sol girl. My dream was to go to Florida. And now, I can't get enough of this place. We're going on a volcano trek at the end of the week to watch the sunrise over Bali and I'm even talking about the magic of temples. Oh god, I'd nearly forgot; Mary has signed me up with her on a Balinese Wisdom course.

'If you'd have told me two weeks ago, that I'd be doing that, I would never have believed you. The thing is; being here, right now at this time has changed me somehow. I'm not sure how it will affect me in the future, but I know I needed this change to happen. I needed to be here.

'And I'm just saying, that if you put yourself out there, in the way that your wife wanted you to, I'll bet you'll get something out of it. You'll be glad you did.

'OK, you're looking at me a little weird now. This must be my cue to shut up.'

Alex was smiling at her, remnants of his tears glistening in his eyes and on his cheeks.

'I was just thinking; something has definitely changed in you. The other night, you hardly said a word all evening, and now look at you. Or should I say, listen to you?'

Josie had finally run out of words. She fidgeted a little then moved further along the tree trunk putting some space between them. She wasn't sure if Alex was teasing or whether she really had gone on too much. He picked up on her uncertainty.

'Hey, I'm only teasing you.' He smiled up at her, his face transformed from the utter despair of a few moments ago. It must be like this all the time for him, she thought.

She smiled back with relief and looked ahead at the gently flowing river.

'So how long have you been here? He asked.

'Almost two weeks. And it's gone so quick.'

'Are you homesick?'

'No. No, actually, I'm not.'

'What about you? Are you going to cut it short and go home?'

'No. I'm going to do what you suggest and give it my best shot; get out there and really experience this place. That's what she wanted me to do.'

Josie smiled, pleased for him. 'Good for you.'

'And how long are you planning to stay now?'

'I should probably say, just one more week. But I know in my heart, I'll stay here in Bali for another four weeks.

Chapter 26

All Hope knew was that Laurie would be brought home from hospital by ambulance sometime that morning.

She sighed for the hundredth time, convinced that if she sucked in any more air, she would hyper-ventilate. Her chest felt tight, and her heart was pounding. She knew she was being ridiculous but couldn't rid herself of the anxiety.

It didn't help that Sara had phoned the night before to say she wouldn't be able to get away for her dad's home coming. Instinctively, Hope knew something was wrong and tried to keep her talking a while, hoping she would eventually confide in her, but Sara wasn't having any of it and kept the conversation short.

The fundamental flaw in the conversation was Sara's attempt at being upbeat and ever so casual about not coming home. The truth was that Sara would have loved to be there when her dad arrived, and it would be breaking her heart that she wouldn't be. She wasn't sure but her daughter sounded close to tears.

Hope replayed the conversation over and over for the rest of the evening and nearly phoned Sara back half a dozen times.

She'd hardly slept all night, her mind being an interminable chatterbox, and now she felt like a zombie; pug-eyed, heavy limbed and clumsy.

She'd bashed her elbow on the door handle, chipped a dinner plate unloading the dishwasher and nearly broken her neck when she'd slipped on Lulu's water bowl that for some reason had moved to the middle of the kitchen floor. Hope had only just managed to stop herself from falling by grabbing onto the back of a chair.

She'd tidied and tweaked every room and then reprimanded herself for bothering. He hardly deserved any of this. He was lucky to even be allowed back in the door. She got up now and went through the kitchen to Laurie's new room in their old dining room. Standing in the open doorway, she looked about. She'd done a good job; it was bright, cosy and comfortable.

A new bed had been delivered a couple of days ago and for some reason Hope had bought new linen for it – it had something to do with feeling separate; she didn't want him to use any of *their* things. And she was glad he had his own washing facilities down here too which meant she had total privacy upstairs. Although, at least at first, he would need help with washing and dressing, and getting in and out of bed. She heard a knock and closed the door on his room, wondering if any of this was going to work out.

In the hallway, she opened the front door.

'Mrs Clements?'

'Yes, that's right.'

'We have a delivery – one husband.' The ambulance driver, probably about the same age as she and Laurie, was smiling broadly. In just a second's thought, she managed to marvel at his cheerful nature despite doing such a demanding job and at the same time be humbled to think of all the silly trivia she deigned to moan about.

Unfortunately, his joke about delivering her husband had been wasted and had gone completely over her head. She felt bad now.

She smiled, as wide as she could manage. 'Yes thankyou, just in here.'

The ambulanceman gave a cheeky salute in acknowledgement and disappeared back to the road. Hope stood in the hallway, by the door, waiting.

Another member of the ambulance team held the gate open as Laurie was wheeled carefully along the now evident very uneven and bumpy garden path. To Hope he suddenly looked very small and not just because he was in a wheelchair, he seemed to have shrunk in stature, he looked shrivelled and tired.

He looked how Hope felt, and within her was an overwhelming urge to run down the path to him and throw herself around him, to hold him tight and give him the energy to recover, for them both to recover and make everything alright.

But she stayed where she was, rooted to the spot, watching as he advanced, unable to say anything or do anything except smile a very weak, unsure smile. As she looked into Laurie's face, he mirrored exactly the same back to her.

It took the cheery ambulanceman some clever manoeuvring to get Laurie and his wheelchair up the front step and into the hallway, and then he did a nifty three-point turn so that Laurie was facing the same way as them.

'OK, there we go. I'll leave you both to it then.'

'Cheers, thanks a lot,' said Laurie.

'Yes, thank-you,' echoed Hope as she watched the ambulanceman dash off, and closed the door behind him.

She didn't know what to do; how to behave or what to say and now the frustration was building together with animosity at Laurie for putting her in this situation. She smiled awkwardly, down at him in his chair. He was clutching the small holdall she'd used to take some of his things to the hospital. He looked completely helpless, and she didn't know how she felt about that.

'Here, let me take that.' She took the bag from his lap and plonked it at the bottom of the stairs. 'Right, where do you want to go? In the living room, or do you want to have a look at your room?'

Laurie gave a small sigh. He looked exhausted and again Hope felt for him, quickly reminding herself that he didn't deserve it.

'In the living room please. That will be great.'

Carefully Hope wheeled him through the doorway, the chair just about fitting through. It was easier than she thought as she'd expected the dead weight of him in the chair to be almost too heavy to move but instead the high-tech wheelchair glided easily over the carpet.

However, it wasn't so easy once they were in the room to actually get him into place. The room was big, but it contained lots of large furniture, making it difficult to move a wheelchair around especially with Laurie's plastered leg outstretched on a support.

Unlike the ambulanceman's nifty three-point turn in their relatively small hallway, Hope now undertook something more like a fifty-point turn to get Laurie into the obvious space between the sofa and the armchair. At first it seemed almost impossible as she wheeled him backwards and forwards then backwards and forwards again, only achieving a few inches nearer to where he needed to be each time. Hope smiled to herself which turned into a giggle, and she was glad she was behind Laurie where he couldn't see her. But he could hear her.

'Are you laughing?'

'No,' she said, trying to contain herself.

'Good, because it would be very distasteful to laugh at a man in a wheelchair.' Laurie wasn't being serious. This was their very normal, very usual silly type of banter. Well, it used to be.

'No, I'm not laughing.' Hope came from behind the armchair to stand in front of him with a perfectly straight face. 'How's that? I think it will be fine for now.' She pulled the low coffee table a little nearer to him, and then pushed the armchair just a shade closer to the open fire, wary of pushing it too close. 'We might have to move things around a bit more, but we can do that another time. You've got easy reach of the table and you can see the tele. Yep, I think that's fine. Ok, a cup of tea I think.' It wasn't a question, and she didn't wait for an answer to that or anything else but turned and hastily left the room, leaving Laurie alone with his own thoughts.

He closed his eyes with utter relief. Thank goodness, he was home at last. And he was also very tired; it had been a very eventful morning. After days spent lying in bed, the whole experience of getting dressed and being moved into the wheelchair and finally being drive home had been exhausting.

He opened his eyes again and looked around him at the comfort and colours of the room as if seeing them for the first time. After the sterile bland brightness of his hospital room, this by contrast was pure luxury. Mostly it had been decorated in neutral colours but always with warmth in them. The vanilla cream of the carpet went well with the more oatmeal shade on the walls and the deep terracotta of the sofa and chairs that matched the curtains brought such a sense of warmth and homeliness to the room, Laurie felt moved to tears. This was all Hope's work; she had a brilliant eye for design.

How lucky was he to have this place for a home? And not only that, but to be able to spend his days working from here. Working, if he could call it that. He knew he hadn't really made much effort over the last couple of years to do anything close to what he knew he was truly capable of. He'd gotten lazy. What a fool he'd been.

Hope returned with two mugs of steaming tea and placed them on the coffee table. She sat across from Laurie on the furthest most seat on the sofa.

'It's great to be home.'

'Is it?'

'Yeah, really great.'

Hope reached forward and took her mug of tea, cradling it in both hands and leaning back as she sipped.

Likewise, Laurie stretched forward to do the same and with some difficulty finally hooked the mug, pulling it towards him. Hope watched, restraining the urge to jump up and help him.

They drank in silence. Hope again restrained herself from feeling obliged to make small talk and fill in the awkward empty silence. Whereas Laurie was simply too tired to talk.

'You must be tired. I know what it's like being in hospital for a while, when all you want is to get home and get on with all the things you'd like to do. And then when you finally get there, you just crash in an exhausted heap.'

Laurie knew what she was referring to. She'd spent nearly three weeks in hospital after a complicated birth with Sara. 'That was different, you came home with a baby to look after.'

'Yes, but you've only got one good leg. And the other isn't that useful. Finish your tea and I'll show you your new room.'

Hope left him alone again and busied herself in the kitchen for a few minutes. When she returned, Laurie's head was drooping, he was almost falling asleep in his tea. She rescued the mug which was just about to topple over in his lap, making him jump a little as she placed it on the coffee table.

She was about to say 'Bed for you' as she would have done at any other time when her husband was unwell or just over-tired and Laurie would have replied with a clichéd suggestive comment and they would have both laughed. But today she stopped herself; it wasn't like that anymore.

'I think you need some sleep.' She made a repeat of the earlier wheelchair dance and felt herself start to laugh again but Laurie was too tired to notice. She managed to get him out of the room slightly more skilfully than before but concluded that it would be far easier if some of the furniture were rearranged. Maybe she'd tackle that tomorrow.

Carefully through the kitchen and into the small adjoining hallway, straight on into Laurie's new room, Hope paused in the doorway so that he could see it all before she pushed him alongside the bed.

From her standpoint behind him, she could see him nodding his head as he looked around the room and she knew that he was pleased with what she'd done. And from the way he swallowed deeply, she also knew that he was choked with emotion. Not an overly emotional man, he'd be glad he had his back to her.

'Did you and Sara do all this, for me?'

Hope winced and couldn't quite face telling him that in fact it was all her hard work. 'Yes, it didn't take us that long.'

'It's perfect Hope, thank-you.'

She allowed him a few moments before gently pushing him into the room and tight up to the side of the bed.

'Ok, do you need me to do anything?' she asked. She knew he would need her help but for all sorts of reasons she didn't want him to rely on her any more than was absolutely necessary.

'I think I can manage most of it,' he said as he expertly lowered the arm of the wheelchair nearest the bed which made it easier to slide out. 'I've been practising this all morning.' He smiled up at Hope who was watching intently as he very deliberately followed the routine he'd learnt just a few hours ago. She knew he would grow to hate this cumbersome routine simply to get in and out of bed.

She stood watching her husband, fighting every natural impulse to rush forward and help. Without thinking about it beforehand, the bed she had chosen for him seemed just the right height for Laurie to shift himself onto it from the chair. As he started to move himself sideways, it was evident that he would need help in lifting his heavily plastered leg along with him. Gently Hope took the weight as he awkwardly shuffled across, supporting himself with his hands on the chair then the bed and his one good leg which was slightly bashed and bruised but not broken.

Finally, he'd made it and lay back, slightly out of breath and closed he eyes.

'Are you in pain?'

'No, I'm OK, thanks. No more pain killers until, I don't know, what time is it?'

'It's nearly midday.'

'A few hours yet, I'll have to work it out.'

'OK, I'll call you for lunch in a while,' she said briskly. He didn't answer and she smiled to see that he was asleep already.

Hope made herself a coffee and went through to the sitting room, sinking down in her favourite armchair by the fire which she'd moved to make way for the wheelchair. She felt a sense of relief now that Laurie was in his room asleep. She was exhausted too. This was not going to be easy. She drank her coffee and shivered; it was very chilly for April and looking out into the garden she could see that the wind was picking up. The laburnum tree just beginning to bud was swaying and dipping, its branches threatening to snap off completely.

She craned her neck to see further; the rose bushes were flipping about wildly and the fence panels were straining with the strength of each hefty gust. Her eyes returned to the laburnum tree, straining against the force of nature. She would be distraught if anything happened to it; they'd bought it the first summer they'd moved into the house – twenty-one years ago. It had been a double celebration, Sara's first birthday and their second wedding anniversary.

She finished her coffee, and propped her feet on the coffee table, closing her eyes for a short nap. She awoke half an hour later, her arm having gone to sleep from resting her head on her hand. And she was cold too. The skies had darkened, and the wind was even stronger now. In the kitchen, she switched the central heating on and turned her thoughts to lunch. It was definitely a hot soup day. There was a time when she could have selected from a range of home-made soups neatly stored in the freezer, but she didn't have time for that anymore. Instead, she rifled through the cupboard and took out a tin of creamy chicken and mushroom soup. There was a part-baked baguette in the freezer, and she placed that in the oven.

While the bread was cooking, it would only take ten minutes, she went through to wake Laurie. Quietly she peeked around the door.

'Laurie. Lunch will be ready soon.'

He didn't move, in fact he had hardly moved at all except for his arm resting across his eyes. Maybe the light had prevented him from sleeping although it was quite dark in there now, and the sharp patter on the garden doors signalled the start of rain.

'Laurie, are you ready to eat?' She called a little louder but still no response. Her gaze moved from Laurie's face down to his chest and then his belly – nothing was moving. In an instant, she was at his bedside, she covered his hand with her own. It was freezing cold. Her heart lurched so violently; a sharp pain shot up through her head.

And then he sighed, moving his arm down from his face although he was still fast asleep. Hope removed her hand from his, observing that it was shaking slightly but she refused to acknowledge any significance of this. Gently she pulled the duvet cover from the other side of the bed and folded it over Laurie. She closed the curtains and quietly closed the door and then returned to the kitchen to eat soup and bread alone.

Chapter 27

Josie had finally immersed herself in the whole wellbeing experience. After her usual solitary breakfast, she went for a walk around the resort gardens, steering clear of the forest river in case Alex went there specifically to be alone.

After that, Mary had the day mapped out with activities for them.

A class of Gentle Yoga had been followed by a short talk on Intuitive Eating and then a Juice Class where they learned how to make healthy smoothies and colourful fruit juice cocktails. She and Mary had lunch together and then relaxed by the pool, chatting for a while.

She had been happy to be guided by Mary's advice on which activities to try but the one thing she resisted was anything to do with meditation. She was worried she wouldn't be able to do it, despite Mary insisting that really there was nothing she actually need to do. The idea was to quiet her mind in order to achieve clarity, but Josie remained adamant – no meditation.

Not entirely ready to give up, Mary suggested a compromise. How about a visualisation exercise? And in case Josie was nervous of being with a stranger, she offered to give the exercise herself.

Josie paused, considering the idea. 'OK then.'

'Wonderful. Let's go to your villa. Bob is watching some sports game he insisted he couldn't miss. Very un-retreat-like but we have to make certain allowances.'

'Your Bob's great. He's very…'

'Tolerant? Is that the word you were looking for?'

Josie laughed. 'Not exactly, no. Patient, maybe. You both have a lovely chemistry or vibe or whatever it is. You're great together, is what I'm saying.'

'Well, thank-you.' Mary was about to ask if this was how she would describe her own partnership with Ross but thought better of it, maybe that was prying a little too far. Although, from the ensuing silence, it was as though the question had been asked, and was lingering in the air. Josie looked very thoughtful.

In no hurry, they strolled through shady pathways making their way to Josie's villa.

'We bumped into Alex this morning while we were taking our early swim. Never seen him in the pool before.'

'How is he? I saw him yesterday; he was incredibly down.'

'Well, he had a lot of good to say about you.'

'Oh, did he? I don't think I did anything to deserve that.'

'He was impressed that the sight of a grown man crying didn't make you run a mile.'

'I can't even imagine what he must be going through.'

'Well, he said you helped him see the true purpose of him being here. Apparently, he's been a bit of a recluse and he's about to make much more effort getting out to see what he can of Bali for the rest of his stay.'

Josie looked surprised. 'Oh. That's fantastic. Good for him.'

'And well done to you too, for helping him along.'

'Oh, I didn't really say much.'

'Sometimes, it's knowing when to say something and when not to that makes all the difference. Sometimes, the best thing is allowing the other person to find the answers themselves.'

'I don't think I did any of that. Just listened, really.'

'Ah, see, you're a natural.'

'A natural what?'

'Listener. Healer maybe. Counsellor maybe. Have you ever thought about taking up any of those things?'

'No, actually, I never have. I couldn't be a counsellor, not me.'

'I disagree. I think you'd be a wonderful counsellor or life coach if you prefer. Give it some thought. Perhaps this is your true purpose for being here in Bali – to find your calling.'

Josie laughed it off. But as they walked along the rest of the way in silence, her mind was already buzzing.

The light had suddenly changed and they both looked up to see a darkened sky just as drops of rain spattered around them.

They quickened their pace; their flip-flops slapping in unison as they marched on, jogging up the steps along the narrow path before finally running as fast as they could the last one hundred yards to Josie's villa.

Once inside, out of breath, rather wet but laughing, Josie grabbed a couple of towels for them to pat themselves dry.

They stood looking out at the rain pelting down on the water in the swimming pool. They glanced at each other and grinned at the incredible noise surrounding them; rain on the wooden roof, water on water in the pool, raindrops splashing into puddles on the decking, and the thunderous drumming of heavy rain on the broad leaves of the forest vegetation.

'Wow! So, this is a tropical storm,' said Josie, loving the sight and sound of it.

Mary was wide-eyed with exhilaration, nodding in recognition of what she'd seen many times before.

'OK, I'm not sure if you'll be able to hear me, but shall we make a start?'

Josie had almost forgotten about the visualisation exercise.

'OK, yes, what do I have to do?'

'Get yourself comfortable, either sitting or lying down. How about over here?'

Mary indicated a comfortable chair further inside the villa at the central dining area, where the sound of rain wasn't quite so loud.

Josie sat down, looking up at Mary for further instruction.

'Just relax, feet flat on the floor, hands in your lap and close your eyes.'

She did as she was told and as she closed her eyes and listened to Mary's soft, soothing voice with the sound of falling rain in the background, she felt her entire body relax easily and effortlessly.

'Now take a few deep breaths, nice and slowly. Try to empty your mind of any busy thoughts or distractions.'

Josie took a deep breath in, and slowly out, aware of her belly rising and falling, as Mary began.

'Imagine yourself in the English countryside. You're in a pretty valley and it's a beautiful summer's day; pale blue skies and sunshine. You can feel the warmth of the sun on your skin as you walk along the fresh summer grass with flowers all around.

'You notice a narrow path and begin to follow it as it gently winds higher up the valley. It brings you to a little brook, crystal clear water rippling over shiny smooth pebbles, and you easily jump across to the other side, climbing higher into the valley.'

Josie sat perfectly still, eyes closed, her breathing relaxed. She was in the valley, could really feel the warm sun on her, and see the trickling brook.

'Now you come to a small, wooded area, and you walk beneath the shade of the trees. It's much cooler here and quiet too, as all sound is absorbed by the dense woodland.

As you stroll along, listening to birdsong and the breeze gently blowing through the leaves, you see a small clearing and a cottage there, a little way off. This cottage can be anything you want it to be, imagine it clearly. What does it look like from the outside? Does it have a garden? Is there smoke coming from the chimney? Is there someone inside waiting for you?'

Josie was completely consumed. She could see her cottage clearly. It was small and pretty, like a pixie's home. It had a dark thatched roof with tiny windows peeking through. Soft golden light shone from all the windows and smoke drifted gently upwards from the chimney.

'Go up to the cottage and walk inside.'

Josie went up the pathway of the pretty little garden and pushed open the door.

'What do you see inside?'

She saw a single room with an open fire blazing away. There was a big comfortable armchair next to it and the room smelled of baking, fresh bread, cinnamon and sugar.

Mary noticed a little smile on Josie's face.

'In the cottage, there is a square table and, on the table, is a box – a present for you. You pick up the present and find somewhere to sit comfortably.'

Josie picked up the small box and sat down in the armchair next to the fire.

'Slowly you unwrap the present.'

Josie noticed that the present she had on her lap wasn't wrapped, it was just a plain white cardboard box.

'Now, take the lid off the box, and there inside is your gift, especially chosen for you.'

Mary paused for a few moments.

'OK, Josie, when you're ready, you can leave the cottage. Take your present with you, of course. Go outside and shut the door. Walk back through the shaded wood and out into the warm sunshine again. Make your way down the valley, across the little brook and back onto the pathway again, taking you further down the valley to the lush grass and the summer flowers, where you began.'

Josie sighed in complete contentment.

'And whenever you're ready, open your eyes.'

She opened her eyes almost immediately and smiled across at Mary.

'My god! That was lovely. Like having a story told to you except I was in the story.'

Mary laughed. 'I'm glad you enjoyed it. What was the best part for you?'

'Arriving at the cottage.'

'Ah yes. Tell me, what was your cottage like? Was it big and grand like your home in England?'

Josie sounded surprised at her findings. 'No actually, it was nothing like it. It was an old cottage, small and cosy, with lots of features and character.'

Mary nodded knowingly.

'And who was waiting for you inside?'

'No-one.' Josie looked at Mary, suddenly seeing a potential significance to the images she'd been seeing. 'There was no-one there, but I didn't mind, I didn't want there to be. There was a single armchair by the fire which I felt was my armchair.'

Mary noticed Josie frowning. 'It's OK, there's no right or wrong to this. It's just a light-hearted relaxation exercise, you can choose to take what you want from it.'

Josie nodded; she was taking a lot from it.

'And what about your present? What was in the box?'

'There was nothing in the box. What does that mean? Does that mean I'll never get anything I want in life?'

'Not at all. What were you expecting as you opened the box?'

'I don't know, I was trying to think so hard, but I couldn't decide what I wanted in the box.'

'Ah, well there you have it. You've just been given a present of whatever you wanted but you couldn't decide. It's the same for a lot of people; they live their lives thinking they never get what they want, but in reality, they don't *know* what they want. You have to decide. You have to choose.'

Josie looked deep into Mary's face. 'Thank you for doing this for me. It's been fascinating. It seems I have a lot of thinking to do. Something's telling me I have to decide what I really want in my life.'

Chapter 28

It was late afternoon and Hope busied herself in the kitchen, very aware of Laurie asleep in the next room. She was trying to be quiet – not so much for his sake as hers; at the moment, it felt easier with him asleep and out of the way. It felt as if there was a stranger in her home.

As she wiped down work surfaces that were already perfectly clean, it suddenly occurred to her that Laurie had no way of calling for help if he needed it. It wasn't something she particularly wanted to think about. She certainly had no intention of being at his beck and call, but they would need to work something out.

She went and listened outside Laurie's room for any signs of movement but it was still quiet and so she gently pushed open the door, peering inside the dark room. It took a moment to focus and when he spoke it made her jump a little.

'Hello.'

'Oh, you're awake.'

'What time is it?'

'Half four, you've slept for a good few hours.'

'Yeah, I was completely out of it.'

'You missed lunch,' she said, immediately regretting the harshness in her voice. She opened the curtains which instead of lighting the room only let the gloomy grey of the outside in. She stood at the bed, looking down on him. 'I can rustle up a bowl of soup if you fancy some.'

'I'm fine. Don't go to any trouble.'

'I won't. It's no trouble, I've already had mine, I've only got to reheat it. You've got to eat.'

'Ok, thanks. That'll be great. I am quite hungry.'

Hope put the soup on to reheat, then stood to the side and leant back against the worktop with her face in her hands. This was exhausting; being angry with him all the time. But she was angry, she couldn't stop that. And yet she hated the sound of it in her voice and in her mind; a biting, snapping, sarcastic voice that was constantly pecking at him. She couldn't keep this up but at the same time, how else could she be?

She stirred the soup, turning the heat down a little. Back in Laurie's room, he'd managed to get himself into a sitting position, and was pulling the wheelchair closer to the bed.

'I wasn't sure if you could do this on your own.'

'I should be able to. I did finally get the hang of it in hospital. It's easier getting in than getting out.'

Hope stood still and watched as Laurie wriggled to the edge of the bed then took his weight with his good leg as he sat in the chair then lifted his plastered leg into place. He smiled up at her, looking quite pleased with himself.

'I should be able to do that the other way around too soon; I'll work on that.'

Hope smiled back. She was pleased; this was one less thing he would rely on her for. Her smile faded as she watched Laurie reach back for his mobile phone on the cupboard next to the bed. She'd like to have a look through that at some point although it was unlikely she would ever get the opportunity. He slipped it into his shirt pocket.

'Right, now let me see if I can drive this thing on my own.' Laurie wheeled himself forward and backwards a few inches, testing his skill. Hope pulled the door right back and watched as he slowly and slightly awkwardly turned towards the hallway. He seemed to be doing fine although it was a very tight fit.

'Ouch, bugger! That hurt.'

'Are you OK? What happened?'

'I bashed my knuckles on the frame.' Laurie was rubbing his hand.

For some reason, Hope laughed. 'Not content with a broken leg and back injuries?'

Laurie made a low grunting noise – she wasn't sure what it meant but she didn't think he saw the funny side.

'Do you want some help?'

'No! Thank-you, but I need to be able to do this by myself.'

Hope stayed behind him and watched him very carefully manoeuvre himself and the wheelchair through the door, just brushing the frame with the backs of his hands. She couldn't help but admire his determination.

Laurie wheeled himself up to the kitchen table while she poured soup into a bowl and put out the remains of the baguette for him.

'Thank-you Hope.' He looked awkward, uncomfortable at having to be waited on, and she left him to eat alone, thinking to herself that no matter what he felt it was nothing compared to her own feelings.

While she was upstairs, she heard Laurie's mobile phone ring and then the low masculine rumble of his voice talking. She crept out onto the landing and listened.

'Hi Roger. Yep, home this morning. It's fantastic to be home.'

Roger was his previous boss before he was made redundant. Their conversation went on for a while and it gave her the excuse to stay out of his way while he was occupied.

After a while she detected that the call had finished, and she met him in the hallway as she came downstairs.

'Thanks for lunch Love, the best food I've had in days. Thanks for doing that.'

She simply smiled in acknowledgement.

'Are you aiming for the living room?'

'That's the idea. I'm coming to the conclusion that we have too many doorways in this house!'

Hope followed him as he positioned himself to where she had pushed him earlier in the day. 'That was Roger on the phone.'

'Ah yes, how's he doing?'

'Yeah, he's good. Just phoned to ask how I was. And would you believe it, they're recruiting again. Isn't that always the way? He wanted to know if I was interested.'

'And are you?'

'It's definitely something to think about.'

It would be, Hope thought, if you didn't have a well-earning wife to look after you anymore.

Laurie looked at her expectantly, interested in her opinion, but she said nothing.

'Do you mind if I put the tele on?'

'No, of course not.'

It was unusual for them both to be home together at this time in the afternoon and if they ever were, it would only be because one of them was dashing in before dashing out again somewhere. Ships passing in the night and all that.

They watched a quiz programme together, each of them occasionally offering up an answer and then before they knew it, they really got into it, competing with each other and laughing at the other's mistakes.

The rain was hammering the windows and it was getting darker by the minute. It felt like Christmas to be sitting in together watching TV. The programme finished and they automatically smiled across at each other.

'Funny,' said Laurie, 'It feels like Christmas; I don't know why it just does.'

'I was just thinking the same. Probably the awful weather outside and it being cosy in here.'

He nodded at the drinks cupboard. 'Shall we have a sneaky afternoon drink? I hear you're into whiskey these days.'

'Hardly. It was just the one.'

She caught Laurie grinning broadly. 'And you'll be glad to know, I still don't like it so don't worry your bottle is safe.'

'So I see, yeah, there's a little dribble left!'

She shook her head, unable to keep the smile off her face.

'Anyway, are you supposed to be drinking, with all your medication and everything?'

'Probably not. But one small one won't hurt. Let's say it's medicinal.'

Hope poured a small measure and topped it up with lots of soda, handing it to Laurie.

She poured a small glass of Baileys for herself. 'Now it really does feel like Christmas.'

She sipped and closed her eyes, savouring the smell and taste of the festive season all in the first creamy mouthful of liquor.

When she opened her eyes, Laurie was holding his glass out towards her.

'Cheers.'

She chinked her glass with his. 'Cheers.'

They had shared numerous times like this but on this occasion neither of them made a toast. They sipped in silence for a few moments, each alone with their own very different thoughts.

'I was thinking to do something simple for dinner - chicken and roast vegetables.'

'Yeah, sounds great. Whatever you think best. Hope don't go to any special trouble for me, I'll be fine with a sandwich, honestly.'

'It's not any trouble. I quite fancy a roast actually.' It was one of the simplest meals to do and she used to cook a roast chicken often but right now she couldn't remember the last time she had.

'It'll be nice to eat together for a change.' Immediately Laurie recognised his words sounded like a criticism. 'I didn't mean anything by that.'

'I know. It's OK.' She was on the verge of agreeing that it would be nice to share a proper meal together, but she didn't.

Hope had drained her glass without realising it. She stood to pour herself another, glancing across at Laurie's glass, pleased to see that he'd hardly touched his drink.

'What's on your mind?' he asked.

'Nothing. Why?' Damn him, for knowing her so well.

'You just seem a bit preoccupied that's all. Wish you were in Bali I suppose?'

'Well yes actually. That's hardly surprising, is it? I bet you do too.'

'What? Wish you were in Bali? Or that I was in Bali?'

He was teasing her, but she was irritated. Her snipe at him and his plans had gone over his head. And she'd ended up just looking silly.

'Actually, there is something on my mind. I've been wanting to say something for a while. And now, well you ought to know too.'

'Oh, this sounds serious.' Laurie straightened himself in the wheelchair and reached to the table for his drink.

As he bent low, Hope watched his anxious face. How worried was he? What did he think she was about to say? That she'd found the divorce papers? It was very tempting. But she was waiting for the right time for that. Maybe when he could walk again and then she could tell him to walk right out of this house and not come back.

She'd decided to tell him about Sara. She wasn't going to carry the burden of that all alone, and he needed to know before she visited again, whenever that was.

'I need to talk to you about Sara.'

His face creased with serious concern. 'What is it? Is she OK?'

'Oh yes, she's fine,' snapped Hope. The look of worry on his face suddenly incensed her. If she'd told him that she had found his secret papers that were about to destroy her life, would he have looked so concerned? In that instant, she doubted it.

'She's not ill, is she?'

'No. She's not ill. She's perfectly well.' Hope snatched herself out of the chair and walked over to the window. She didn't want to see him, didn't want to even be able to look at him. She wanted him to hurt, the way she was hurting. She wanted him to feel what it was like to be betrayed by someone you thought loved you and was honest with you.

Hope looked down the length of the garden to the trees at the end, swooping and bending, relentlessly buffeted by the wind, tortured by their incessant battering. At what point would they finally break?

She turned to face her husband.

'What is it Hope?'

She sighed deeply and returned to the armchair next to Laurie. At some point she would make the opportunity to talk to Laurie. But using Sara to cause him pain wasn't the right way, she knew that. What she had to tell him, would cause anguish enough without her twisting the knife.

She cradled the glass of Baileys in both hands, warming the creamy liquid. She took a deep breath. Now the moment had come to discuss what she'd known for over a year, suddenly she didn't know where to start.

'She's dropped out of university.'

'What? Why? Why's she gone and done that? She was doing brilliantly. When did this happen?'

'Well, we have only just talked about it.'

'But she never said anything, when she visited me in hospital.'

Hope was suddenly mortified with herself for having known about this for well over a year and not saying anything to Laurie. He obviously thought this had all happened within the last few days or so. How on earth was she going to explain?

'As I said, we've only just talked about it. But actually, I've known something – not the whole story – but I knew she'd left about a year ago.'

'What! You've known for a year and never said anything to me. Why?'

'Because I didn't really know anything to tell. I found out by accident. I was waiting for Sara to actually tell me, but she never did. And I thought maybe you knew anyway.'

'Why would I know?'

'Because you and Sara, you know, you've always been so close. I thought she may have confided in you.'

Laurie rubbed his hand over the back of his neck, squeezing the taught tendons as if to ease their tension. He sighed, shaking his head and seemed lost for words. He spoke quietly.

'Of course we're close. She's my daughter, my only child. But I don't think she would have confided in me over you. And, do you know what?' Laurie looked up, square into her face. 'If she had told me, I would have told you.'

Hope cast her eyes down into her drink. She could feel her face burning with shame. She knew that everything Laurie had said was true; he wouldn't keep a secret between him and Sara from her.

'For god's sake Hope, how did we get to this?'

She looked across at him. 'That's a loaded question.'

Their eyes met, just a short distance from each other and yet further apart than they'd ever been.

He looked sad. 'We stopped talking. We got too busy for each other.' Laurie took a glug of his drink and placed the glass on the table.

Hope listened, noting there was no hint of accusation in his voice. But something stirred deep within her, an iota of guilt in the pit of her stomach. They both knew that it was she who had got too busy, with her writing, the shop, general business matters.

'So, OK, you've known for a while. How did you find out?'

'One of her housemates told her mother about my books. And she contacted me, the mother that is, and asked for a couple of signed copies. I sent them off, she phoned to thank me, we got chatting of course and then she mentioned what a shame it was that Sara had left university.'

'And that was the first you'd heard?'

Hope smiled ironically and nodded.

'That must have been tough.'

'I felt such an idiot. I just didn't know what to say.'

'What did you say?'

'I just bluffed my way, saying it wasn't a good time for her, bla, bla, bla.'

'And is that the only reason she gave to you? That it isn't a good time, whatever that means.'

'No, that was me, just making some silly excuse. She told me why she left.' Hope looked at Laurie, the concern in her face now. 'You'd better brace yourself; you haven't heard the worst.'

Laurie twisted round in his wheelchair as best he could to face her, wincing with the pain in his back.

'She's living with somebody,' she said rather vaguely.

'Somebody? A man? Or is she…?'

'No. Yes, it's a man!' Hope sighed. 'The thing is - a much older man. One of her lecturers, a professor actually.'

'Christ! How old is he?'

'Not that old, late thirties.'

'When you said Professor.'

'I know, it makes him sound ancient.'

'Bloody hell, he's almost the same age as me.'

Hope nodded, letting it all sink in for Laurie.

'There's more isn't there?'

'He's married. Separated, but still married. And he has children. I did ask but she wouldn't say any more. That's all I know.'

Laurie had covered his face with his hands, suddenly bringing them down and thumping the arms of the wheelchair, fists clenched, his face red with anger.

'Maybe it's a good thing I'm stuck in this chair.' He was shaking his head as if in total disbelief.

'So she's given everything up, to shack up with him? Just like that?'

'I think the intention is to continue with her studies. She mentioned finding another university. And this,

Sam's his name, is supposed to be helping her find somewhere.'

Laurie snorted. 'She left a year ago? He hasn't done much for her so far has he? I take it she left to protect his reputation. Tongues wagging, were they?'

'I think so, something like that.'

'It wouldn't go down too well would it, when they hear that one of the teachers has shacked up with his pupil.'

'Laurie, she is twenty-two, not exactly a child.'

'Even so. You know what I mean.'

'Yes, I do. I know what you mean.'

There was silence between them while they were both deep within their own thoughts.

'What do we do now?' he asked.

'Not much we can do. Support her, encourage her to continue studying.'

'Be there for when it all comes crashing down.'

'Well, we don't know that it will. I was married at her age.'

'Oh come on, kids aren't ready for the kind of responsibility we had at her age. It's completely different now.'

Again, Hope nodded in agreement. Laurie drained his glass.

'Would you mind getting me another drink Love?' She looked at him with reproach. 'I need another drink, just a small one.'

Hope poured him another tiny measure of whiskey with lots of soda.

Chapter 29

It was a Monday morning in mid-April, the beginning of Josie's third week in Bali. Bob and Mary had gone on a day trip to the village of Sekumpul in the north of the island. They were planning to go for a nature walk through a bamboo forest and then to take in the sights of its spectacular waterfalls. Alex was going along with them; his holiday was almost finished, and they had already said their good-byes, wishing each other well.

Josie was invited too but she'd declined, feeling the need to spend some time alone.

After her usual routine of breakfast and a walk, she'd added the healthy habit of a quick swim in her own pool. And then she would shower in the villa's open-air bathroom, something she didn't think she'd ever be brave enough to use when she first arrived, even though it provided complete privacy for the villa's resident.

She'd come to relish the feeling of showering, completely naked, out in the elements, looking up to the sky and the forest beyond, as she washed her hair.

She was gradually working her way through the resort's menu of treatments and today she'd booked herself a Javanese Royal Lulur Bath.

The treatment began with a soothing massage followed by a body scrub using an aromatic mix of spices. Josie was immediately aware of how much more easily she was able to relax into it compared to the day of her first ever massage when her mind had been a swirling tornado.

Next, she was treated to an application of cooling yoghurt on her skin, followed by a long relaxing soak in a warm bath filled with exotic flowers in vibrant colours of pink and gold.

As she lay in the water, surrounded by flower heads dancing around her, she rested her head back and allowed her thoughts to return once again to the visualisation exercise given by Mary just a few days before.

She kept thinking about the little cottage she'd seen and the significance of no-one being at home except her. She thought of Ross and their enormous modern home and felt nothing for it. It wasn't homely, it was soulless.

She and Ross had continued to exchange text messages, but something wasn't right. Something was missing. And she was coming to the conclusion that it had never really been right and that something had always been missing.

She sighed, and gently scooped a large pink flower head into her hand, letting the water drain away through her fingers. She held it close to her face, marvelling at the miracle of its perfection before lowering it back onto the water.

Since the visualisation exercise, she'd felt noticeably calmer and more relaxed, and she knew it had been Mary's slightly sneaky introduction to the whole meditation thing. But she didn't mind. She was intrigued by it all; these exercises of the mind and the insights they could provide.

She closed her eyes, completely relaxing in the warm, scented water. In her mind, she thanked Mary for introducing her to these new experiences. And she thanked whatever the powers might be for bringing Bob and Mary into her life, for she felt certain they would be lifelong friends.

And whatever the powers were for getting her to Bali in the first place, mostly she had to thank Hope for persuading her to come. She would be eternally grateful for that.

She was here for another three weeks, and then what? She'd learnt so much already and could feel a subtle change within her that she liked. And there was so much more to learn.

Chapter 30

Hope had spent the morning in the kitchen cooking a bulk batch of chicken and leek soup. With Martha minding the shop and no writing deadlines to work to, she'd never had so much time to herself. Of course, she was at home under the guise of looking after Laurie, but in reality, she left him to cope on his own as much as he could. And, in all fairness, he was doing very well.

He'd been home for almost a week and somehow, they had found a way of chugging along together, focusing on life's daily essentials and developing routines that kept them both occupied.

The simple things like having breakfast together, mid-morning coffee in the garden if it was warm enough, and an evening meal together, made Hope realise how little time she had been spending at home up until Laurie's accident. And she was enjoying it, despite being acutely aware of the irony of the situation.

Talking to Laurie about Sara had been good. It was a cliché, but she felt a weight lift from her shoulders since talking to him and offloading some of the burden she'd kept to herself for so long.

Every now and then, she noticed Laurie in front of the television, deep in thought, paying no attention whatsoever to the programme he was supposed to watching. She guessed his thoughts were with his daughter and whatever was going on up in Leicester.

Sara said she'd be home in a few days, but Hope was still uneasy about how long it had taken for her to come down to visit her dad now that he was home. This wouldn't be her decision. Something wasn't right.

Laurie had his first physiotherapy appointment yesterday morning, coming home with a pair of crutches to start working with. She couldn't help but admire his determination to be as independent as possible. She needn't have worried about having to fetch and carry for him, if it were at all possible to do something for himself, he would do it.

He'd been practicing with his crutches the day before and again this morning but when he tried to take the stairs by himself, she'd actually insisted that he allow her to help him. The thought of him tumbling back down the stairs had her shaking her head with disbelief. What was he thinking? She helped him along to his workroom and told him to call for her when he was finished.

Back in the kitchen she began to think of their evening meal, she wanted to attempt something a little more adventurous for a change. She realised how much she missed thinking about grown-up food, focusing as she had done on children's cookery skills for so long.

Today she was going to make a duck cassoulet. She and Laurie particularly liked French food and this was something she hadn't done before. Before long, the aroma of duck legs sizzling in the frying pan meandered through the downstairs rooms, while she prepared stock and beans.

It was baffling to her how she could, on occasion, so completely zone out of what she'd discovered in the attic and put it to one side allowing the loving, caring wife to do her thing.

She had become a split personality, being pulled as if in a tug-of-war, a few inches this way and then a few inches back in the opposite direction, never quite knowing second by second what she would feel or who she would be.

She'd wanted to set the table nicely with candles and their best crystal glasses, but she decided not to after all.

Laurie had been upstairs while she was preparing dinner and eventually, she sent him a text message asking him if he was finished. She thought it was quite funny – sending texts within the same house and expected a witty reply, but Laurie just answered 'OK'.

It seemed more difficult coming down the stairs than going up and Hope wasn't sure if Laurie was being awkward by not allowing her to help him so much this time.

With Laurie seated at the kitchen table, she dished the meal.

'Was it nice being back in your work room?'

'Yeah, it was,' Laurie answered, without much enthusiasm.

'And, everything, how you left it?' Hope could have kicked herself for asking what must appear to be a very odd question. She didn't hear Laurie answer and looked up to see him staring at the table, simply nodding as his response.

The duck cassoulet was delicious and provided a safe subject to immerse themselves in, although Laurie was still a little subdued. After they'd finished eating, Hope stacked the dishwasher and left Laurie to hobble on his crutches into the living room. She could hear him getting cross and what sounded like one of his crutches falling onto the table, but she stopped herself from running in to help.

Once she'd finished tidying in the kitchen, she joined him and sat in her armchair next to him. He still used his wheelchair which made it easy to rest his leg. It was a particularly chilly evening and she'd lit a fire which was burning nicely.

Suddenly, Hope cocked her head to one side.

'What is it?'

'I thought I heard a car, on the drive. No, maybe not.'

Laurie was just about to put the television on when they heard a key in the lock of the front door which then burst open with the sound of Sara swearing under her breath.

Hope and Laurie looked at each other in surprise, as she appeared in the living room. Hope was immediately out of her chair.

'Hello. I didn't know you were coming today.'

'I don't have to ask permission do I, to come home?'

'Well, no, of course not.'

Sara slammed her keys down onto the side table. Laurie looked on, as if his daughter were a stranger.

'I'm just saying it would have been nice to know, and then we could have been more prepared, that's all.'

'Well thanks Mum, but I don't want to be treated like a visitor, like a stranger. Or are you telling me this isn't my home anymore?'

'That's enough Sara!' This was Laurie. Voice raised. At his daughter. 'Don't you dare speak to your mother like that. She's had enough to deal with, looking after me in this state.'

'Don't worry! I know where I'm not wanted! I didn't mean to get in your way.'

Sara snatched up her keys, stomped out to the hallway, slamming the front door shut behind her.

Laurie and Hope looked at each other, questioningly and helplessly. She started to go after her. She was sure it was what Laurie would expect her to do.

'Leave her Hope.'

'But what was that all about? Something's up.' They heard Sara's car start up, revving aggressively.

'She's not a kid anymore. If she wants us to know that, then she can't come in here and have a temper tantrum whenever she feels like it, expecting us to jump.'

Hope sat back down. Stunned. She'd never heard Laurie talk like that.

And then they both heard a terrible thud and the crunch of metal.

Hope jumped up. 'Oh my god! What's she done now?' She looked through the curtains out onto the drive.

'Oh no! She's reversed into the tree.'

Hope dashed out the front door, as Laurie struggled to get to his feet as quickly as he could. Hope pulled the driver's door open to see Sara bent over the steering wheel, thankfully uninjured but with her face in her hands, sobbing uncontrollably.

She encouraged her out of the car, and although instinctively she knew that her crying was nothing to do with her driving into a tree, her car being stacked full of boxes and bags of her things was a telling clue. She hugged her daughter who was shaking with emotion, noticing at the same time, Laurie standing with the help of his crutches at the front door.

'Go back inside Sara. Go on, look, Dad's waiting for you.'

Sara looked behind her at the car, a sad look on her face as if it were a broken toy.

'Don't worry about that. I'll move it back onto the drive. Go on, go inside.'

Sara walked wearily towards the house as Hope jumped into the car and carefully drove onto the drive, parking it tightly behind her own car.

Back in the house, Sara was perched on the edge of the settee, staring into space. Laurie was standing helplessly behind her. Hope returned to the room dumbfounded by the scene in front of her; the distance between father and daughter felt immense. After years of feeling like the outsider, was it now up to her to bring them both together?

Laurie nodded at the drinks cabinet. 'I was thinking, a small whiskey, for all of us.' He looked over at Sara who hadn't said a word.

'OK, but go and sit back down,' she said quietly. 'You're not supposed to stand for too long.'

Laurie lowered himself back into his wheelchair while Hope poured some drinks. She handed one to Sara, but she shook her head.

'Go on, it's got lots of soda in it. It'll make you feel better, for a while anyway, I can vouch for that.' Hope laughed at herself and managed to get a little smile out of Sara.

She sat next to her on the settee, took hold of her free hand and simply held it. There was no need to say anything, not right now. And in such a short time, Sara seemed to have burnt herself out; anger and frustration gone, she was calm now and totally worn out.

'It's good to see you home, Dad.'

'Thanks Love. It's good to be home.'

Hope got up and put her drink on the table. 'How about I go run you a hot bath? Then something for supper and an early night?'

Sara nodded gratefully, feeling tears welling up again, although for a very different reason this time.

'Do you need anything from your car?'

Sara shook her head and followed her mum upstairs.

When Hope returned, Laurie sheepishly indicated his empty glass.

'Here have mine, I still don't like whiskey. I'll get myself a glass of wine.'

They chatted quietly, speculating on exactly what had happened in Sara's world that evening. They would find out soon enough.

They could hear her moving around upstairs and soon she reappeared in the living room, bundled up in a pink towelling bathrobe, her hair wet and pulled back from her face which was unusually completely free of make-up, scrubbed clean and rosy pink. She looked like a little girl.

'I'm off to bed,' she said wearily.

'Let me get you something to eat.'

'No, it's OK Mum. Thanks anyway. I'm not hungry. Just tired.'

'OK, we'll see you in the morning. Night-night.'

'Night. Night Dad.'

'Goodnight Sweetheart. See you in the morning.'

Sara left the room. Hope and Laurie looked at each other, helplessly, and smiled lovingly. Hope felt like crying herself, for all sorts of reasons. How she would love to go to him right now, kneel down at his feet, have him hold her, kiss her, and tell her everything would be alright.

He picked up on her sadness.

'Hey! She'll be fine. We'll get her through it.'

'I know.'

Laurie reached across the little distance between them and tickled her fingertips with his own, and then squeezed her hand.

She looked up into his kind face, aware of how much she was still attracted to him. He was a very attractive man. And then she looked away, unlocking their hands, and looked down into the flames of the fire.

'I know about the divorce papers.'

She expected shock, some uncomfortable fidgeting and quick-thinking excuses.

'I know,' is all he said.

And it was Hope who was shocked, snapping her face around to look at him.

'How? How do you know?'

'The key. The key to the drawer that was locked. I always put it back the same – north to south.' He smiled weakly at his own fussy particular ways. 'I always put it back in the same position, north-south, and you replaced it east to west.'

Hope just stared at him, almost unbelieving.

'And the documents were a little jumbled up too. They weren't in the same order.'

'You and Martha.'

'No Hope, there is no me and Martha.'

Here we go, she thought. But she was listening, in fact, hanging on his every word.

Laurie breathed in deeply, psyching himself up for what he felt was the most important conversation of his life.

'But you both went away together, for the weekend. Just a few weeks ago?'

Laurie looked dismal. 'Yes, we did. It was the only time though. And I know that doesn't make it alright. Before that, we'd just been spending time together.'

'But you wanted to divorce me. That's why you told me to come to the pub that night.'

'I didn't want to divorce you. I wrote those documents out ages ago. In a fit of temper. We were hardly seeing anything of each other Hope, and last year when I wanted to celebrate our wedding anniversary, try to get things back on track? You didn't even want to know. There was nothing from you. I snapped, downloaded the forms from the internet and filled them in, got it all out. I never had any intention of doing anything with them, not really.'

'But you wanted me to meet you, the night before I was going to Bali, the night of your accident. What was that all about?'

'I was going to suggest some time apart, that's all. You were off to Bali for six weeks anyway.'

'And you were going to shack up with Martha?'

'No, no way. I was going to stay with Roger. I confided in him that we were having problems. He has a self-contained flat above his garage; we were just talking about it, that's all.'

'I know she's been visiting you in hospital.'

He nodded. 'Only a couple of times. I asked her to stop coming.'

'She was pretending to be your sister, to hospital staff.'

'I didn't know that. I think she's lonely. Not that it makes any of this right. I've told her it's over. It was over before it even began.'

'How come she hasn't been around to visit you here?'

'She wanted to; I told her 'no'. I said you were here, and it wasn't right.'

'And what now? You still want some time apart?'

'No, I don't. This last week has been, well, amazing. We've spent so much time together, like we used to. We were losing each other Hope. This week has been like getting to know each other again.'

He held out his hand towards her, but she didn't take it. She was thinking back over the last few days, and she had to admit she'd thoroughly enjoyed being at home and despite everything, how she'd enjoyed being around Laurie, and just doing the ordinary everyday things together.

She'd been so preoccupied with work and the business over the last couple of years, it was true, everything else had taken a back seat.

Laurie was still holding out his hand.

'What about you Hope, what do you want?'

'I want things to go back as they were,' her words were barely audible.

'No, not as they were. I'm thinking, better than they've ever been.'

She gazed at his outstretched hand and finally placed hers inside it.

Chapter 31

Sara had been home for a couple of days, staying mostly in her bedroom and only coming out for meals. She would then help clear away before disappearing again.

Hope was happy to give her some space to herself, to let her brood and lick her wounds but today they would talk. And also, Hope had plans for herself and she needed Sara's help.

Laurie was up in his attic office, and she and Sara had just had boiled eggs for breakfast. Sara was about to unload the dishwasher of last night's dinner things.

'Leave that Love, come and sit down. Let's have another coffee.'

Like a robot, Sara went to the table and sat down. She knew this time would come. Hope made two mugs of coffee and sat next to her daughter.

'How are you feeling now?' Sara was still in her nightclothes, a big baggy t-shirt and her towelling robe flopping around her. She looked a sad, sorry sight.

'I'm OK,' she said unconvincingly.

'Have you had any contact with Sam, over the last few days?'

Sara shook her head. 'I never want to hear from him or see him again.' She hung her head, crying silently. Hope placed her hands over Sara's on the table and waited. Sara sighed and shuddered at the same time.

'I suspected something was wrong for a long while. You get to know someone, don't you?'

'Yes, you do.'

'And you can feel it when they start being distant, keeping you at arm's length. It's horrible.'

Hope rubbed her back gently. Suddenly Sara looked up at her mum as if in apology.

'It's why I didn't come home when dad came out of hospital. I didn't want to leave him – I didn't trust him. I'm sorry Mum. Dad must have thought I was horrible.'

'Of course he didn't. It's OK. You have your own life to get on with.'

'Yeah, right. I don't have a life.'

Hope smiled. Here was a hint of the daughter she knew; the self-pitying, stroppy one, although she suspected this version of her was definitely on the way out.

Suddenly, Sara laughed. 'I sound like a stupid teenager, don't I?'

Hope grinned back and nodded. And then they both laughed. Sara's nose was running, and she wiped it on the back of her hand.

'Get a tissue!' Hope laughed more, as Sara defiantly wiped her nose on the sleeve of her bathrobe.

'You're disgusting!'

Their laughter subsided as quickly as it had started, and Sara continued.

'This is such a cliché; I feel so stupid. I'd gone off to work as usual in the morning, earlier this week after we'd had all that really heavy rain. Anyway, the shop was totally flooded. We all stayed to help for a bit but then we were sent home. And when I got to the flat, he was there with someone else. I don't even know who she was.'

'Oh Sara, it must have been awful.'

She was crying again, nodding her head. Hope grabbed a box of tissues from the dresser and put them on the table in front of Sara.

'He said it didn't mean anything. Although, he didn't even bother to be that convincing.'

Hope had been cautious not to say anything that might lead to confrontation.

'You've been very brave to move out. It can't have been an easy decision.'

'I had to. It's the worst thing a man can do, isn't it, to a woman he says he cares about. They just don't get it, do they?'

'Yes, it is. It's the worst thing.'

Sara took a deep breath. She blew her nose and sniffed, wiped her eyes and face.

'So, then I went and stayed with a friend, someone I work with at the shop, for a couple of days, then went back and got all my stuff. And came back here.'

She looked up at her mum, and smiled as if admitting defeat, the very beginnings of a sense of relief about her. 'Shall we have another coffee?'

After another coffee and a little more chat, Hope stood up.

'Right, no hiding in your bedroom today. You need to get washed and dressed because I need your help.'

Sara looked intrigued. 'OK.'

'There are going to be some changes in this house. I'd like to reduce my working hours and to start with, that Martha woman has got to go.'

Sara's eyebrows shot up in surprise. 'Oh goody! I never did like that woman.'

'You never said.'

'You never asked.'

'Let's not go there.'

'What do you want me to do?'

Hope had phoned Martha on the pretext of asking about business. They'd chatted for a few minutes, and Hope had made a special point of telling her that she felt terribly guilty. She'd spent so much time with Laurie over the last few days, she had hardly visited her mother. But now that Laurie was getting better and was much more mobile, she'd decided to spend the whole afternoon at her mother's house. In fact, she would be leaving shortly to go and have lunch with her.

Sara had been given strict instructions to drive to the High Street, hide in her car and when she saw Martha leave the shop, she was to phone her mother. She was then to go into the shop herself and find a local locksmith to come and change the locks immediately.

Hope was sitting in a teashop just a few minutes' drive away; with a pot of tea and a Danish pastry that she had no appetite for. Her stomach churned and her heart raced as she waited for the call. Finally, her mobile buzzed on the table.

'Mum, it's me!'

'Yes, why are you whispering?'

'I don't know. Why am I hiding in my car, just about to change the locks on the shop?'

'I already said, I'll explain later.'

In truth, Hope had no idea what she would explain later to Sara.

'Ok, well, she's just left. I'll wait to see her drive off then I'll go in.'

'Good. And don't forget the alarm will start beeping.'

'Yes, I know, I've got the code written here.'

'Ok. Good. Now, you're to stay there, until I phone you.'

'Right. This is really weird Mum.'

'I know. I've got to go. I'll speak to you soon.'

Hope drove back home, parked a little distance away and walked quickly to the house. She'd left Laurie stretched out on the settee watching a film, with instructions for him not to move around unless he absolutely had to. It was a bright, sunny day and she'd closed the living room curtains supposedly to block the sunlight from the TV screen.

Then she'd gone to his downstairs bedroom and unlocked the French doors. With all the plotting and precision planning, she felt like a desperate criminal.

She opened the garden gate now, and quietly hurried to the house, noting the curtains still closed in the living room. She opened the French doors, letting herself in to Laurie's makeshift bedroom and waited there for what felt like forever.

And then she heard it. A knock at the front door. She opened the bedroom door, listening as Laurie hauled himself off the settee, muttering and swearing as he struggled to get up.

The caller knocked again, more loudly and insistent.

'OK, OK, I'm coming. And you better not be selling anything.'

That's interesting, thought Hope, he obviously isn't expecting anyone. She tiptoed into the little hallway and hid by the kitchen door, listening. She heard the front door open.

'Martha. What are you doing here?'

'What do you think? I wanted to see you.'

'You shouldn't be here. Hope could be back any minute.'

Martha stepped into the hallway and closed the door.

'No she won't. She phoned me; told me she'd be at her mother's all afternoon.'

There was silence for a few seconds and then their voices were quieter. They must have gone into the living room, thought Hope, as she slowly made her way through the kitchen. She'd be in trouble now if he suddenly decided to make Martha a cup of tea although judging from the sound of his voice, he certainly wasn't encouraging her to stay.

She crept out into the main hallway and hid by the stairs and heard Laurie sigh heavily.

'Look Martha, I'm really sorry about what's happened. I enjoyed your company and your friendship in the beginning, but it wasn't supposed to get to this point. This has to end. Right now. I'm sorry, I didn't mean for anyone to get hurt.'

'Someone always gets hurt in these situations. But don't worry, it won't be me. Wait until your wife gets to hear about this.'

'She already knows Martha.'

'And don't tell me, you want to stay with her? How pathetic. We could have had a good life together Laurie. I could've had full control of the shop and internet business. I'd make a better job of it on my own.'

'But that's Hope's business, she'd never give that up.'

'She might not have any choice, in a divorce settlement.'

'We're not getting divorced Martha and even if we did, I would never go after her business. She's worked all her life for that. This is over Martha. I want you to leave.'

Hope could hardly breathe, she put her hand to her chest, her heart was pounding so heavily, she was sure they'd be able to hear it in the next room. Tears were prickling her eyes, but she wouldn't allow them – not yet. There was still one more thing she needed to do.

She strode into the living room. All eyes were on her, but Laurie spoke first.

'Hope, I thought you were at your mother's.' He looked frantically from Hope to Martha and back again, instantly aware of how this would look.

Hope could see the panic on his face and walked towards him. With Martha now behind her, she smiled at Laurie, a deep knowing smile that he read in an instant. She stood next to her husband and faced Martha.

'I think you've been asked to leave once already.'

Martha prickled on the spot, throwing dirty looks in every direction.

'And I want you to leave the business too. We can sell the shop, or you can buy me out. We can do this reasonably amicably or we can get solicitors involved. Up to you.'

Martha shot her a look, but knew she was on the losing team. She clutched her handbag tight to her shoulder, looked down her long nose at both of them and walked out, slamming the front door behind her.

Hope collapsed down into the armchair, head in hands. 'I don't think that's the last we've seen of her.'

Laurie plonked himself down on the settee, his crutches left to fall to the floor. 'It'll be alright; I'll do everything I can to sort this mess. Crikey, she was nutty.'

Hope looked up, and they laughed in relief. Laurie looked exhausted.

'I just hope she doesn't hot-foot it down to your shop and do anything stupid.'

'I've taken care of that; Sara's there now and I've asked her to get someone in to change the locks.'

Laurie stared down at his hands, they were sweating, and he wiped them on his jeans. 'You mean you got her out of the way, so she didn't have to hear all this.'

'Yes, that too. But I did need her – I couldn't be in two places at once. And, no, she doesn't need to hear this. She's got enough to deal with at the moment. This is just between you and me.'

'Thank-you, Hope, thank-you for that.'

'Wow, this is the best; fish and chips and champagne. What a way to live.'

Hope and Laurie exchanged smiles; it was wonderful to see their daughter smiling again. She'd never been inside her mum's cookery shop before and hadn't stopped talking about it all afternoon.

She'd called a local locksmith and had the locks changed and while she waited, as instructed, for her mum to call her, she had a good look around.

'There's so much more you could do with the place Mum. You could give demonstrations, on Saturday mornings perhaps, people love things like that. You could make a whole morning of it, you know, offer a glass of wine, some nibbles.'

'I have enough to do without committing my Saturday mornings, thank you very much. Anyway, as I said before, I'm cutting my work hours not adding to them.'

She looked across at Laurie who nodded at her and smiled.

'I'm just saying, it has so much potential, it would be a real shame to sell the place, especially to that crazy woman. The shop is only the success it is because of your writing. And actually, if you let me have a look at the books, I'll do a proper financial assessment for you. I did actually go to university for a couple of years – I did learn a few things.'

'OK, I'll get them out for you tomorrow.'

Laurie picked up his champagne glass to give a toast. He looked questioningly at Hope who simply gave him a look back which said, 'mind your own business, I have a plan in mind' and then she gave him a cheeky wink.

Laurie held his glass high; Hope and Sara did the same. But Sara got in first.

'Cheers everyone, it's always good to come home. Here's to happy lives, love and laughter to us all.'

Epilogue

One month later

Hope popped her head around the living room door. 'Ok, dinner's ready, you can come in now.'

Sara followed her through the kitchen together with Laurie who could hobble along much easier now he had a smaller cast on his leg. They went into the newly decorated dining room and sat down at the table which was laid out with a full beef roast dinner.

'Wow, that's a big bottle of champagne Mum.'

'Mm, that's because we have a lot of celebrating to do. First of all, of course, Dad's new job.'

Sara sneaked a small roast potato from the dish and Hope pretended to smack her hand away.

'So, are you nervous Dad, about starting a new job, you know, after not working all this time?'

'Yes, I am a little I suppose. But looking forward to it too.'

'So, this is kind of weird; Dad will be out at work all day, and Mum, you'll be spending more time at home.'

'I won't be out every day. I'll be working from home a couple of days a week, and your mum is going to spend more time writing from home, so hopefully, it's all going to work out great.'

Hope smiled across at Laurie. 'Are you going to carve, or shall I?'

'I'll do it.'

'You've done a great job with the dining room, Mum. I love the colours.'

Now that Laurie was sleeping back upstairs, Hope had wasted no time in redecorating the dining room, determined that they would start using it more often, especially now that Sara was permanently living back home.

She'd had the walls painted a soft grey and had bought a new table and chairs of solid and chunky, whitewashed effect wood – much less formal than before, giving a slightly rustic feel to the room.

Laurie carved the beef and then everyone helped themselves to vegetables and gravy.

'I got an email from Josie this morning,' said Hope.

'Oh yeah, how's she doing?' asked Laurie.

'Great, she sounds so happy.'

'This is your friend who took your place in Bali?' said Sara.

'Yes, that's right.'

'I don't think I've ever met her. She should be back soon, shouldn't she?'

Hope smiled. 'I'm not sure if she's ever coming back.'

'She's staying in Bali?'

'No, she stayed there for the whole six weeks and now she's in Florida. She made some friends in Bali, from the States – Florida, and apparently, their daughter runs a residential study centre for alternative therapies. Josie has signed up for three months – all charged to her husband's credit card! Good for her, I say!'

'Wow, that's a serious lifestyle change,' said Sara.

'And talking of lifestyle changes, I think we should open the champagne.'

Laurie looked up, recognising his cue, he took the champagne from the ice bucket, and began uncorking it. Hope continued.

'Sara, what do you think to this? I've decided not to sell the shop after all.'

'Really? You've had some good offers, what's changed your mind? I thought you wanted to spend more time writing, less time in the shop.'

'That's exactly what I do want. I've made Martha an offer for her share which she has accepted, and I'd like to give that share over to you, all done properly in your name and everything. I'll still be the majority shareholder, but I'll be a silent partner. I want you to take complete charge and run it as your own business. Does that interest you?'

'Does that interest me? Mum, I can't believe it.'

At that second, the cork burst out of the champagne bottle and hit the ceiling, as the bubbly fizz frothed over the bottle. Laurie quickly filled everyone's glass and raised his in the air.

'That's a yes then Sara?'

'Yes, yes, it's a great big yes!'

'Cheers then,' said Laurie.

'Cheers,' echoed Sara.

'Cheers,' said Hope. 'And here's to happy lives, lots of laughter, and always love.

I hope you enjoyed reading Live Laugh Love and if you did, I would be very grateful if you would leave me a review on Amazon, letting me and other readers know what you think.

Thank you very much,
Jennie

www.JennieAlexander.co.uk

If you enjoyed reading Live Laugh Love, read on for a sample of a lovely story of new beginnings and friendships galore!

A Nice Glass of Red

Chapter 1

November

Winnifred Mayhew clicked off her phone and returned to the living room, smiling to herself and shaking her head as she sank back down onto the over-sized squashy sofa.

Doug looked up from where he was crouching at the wood-burning stove.

'Thought I'd get the fire going, there's a bitter wind out there this evening.'

'Yes, good idea.'

'And I poured you a nice glass of red – thought you might need it.'

'Mm, lovely.' Winnifred took a sip and replaced the glass on the table, recognising immediately the full-bodied Cabernet Sauvignon, savouring its dark fruit flavours and herbal notes.

Doug looked over at his wife as she leant back, eyes closed, contented, still smiling.

'I take it, it was a good call? And what are you grinning at?' He sat down heavily in his armchair right next to the fireplace, pleased with his efforts to get the fire going, and cradled his whisky glass in both hands, full attention now on his wife.

'Oh, they just make me laugh that's all. I've been meeting up with my friends from work every six months, for what is it, over twenty years? And, I swear, for the last ten we've done exactly the same thing. It's so frustrating.'

'And why's that a problem now? I'd say it's amazing you agree on doing something you all enjoy.'

'Well, that's just it; it would be nice to do something different for a change. I think it's got to the point where no-one likes to suggest anything new. We're probably all sitting there hating pizza and pasta with a passion!'

'Why don't you suggest something?'

'I did. I was talking with Esther just then – it's her turn to organise the evening. I recommended the new Thai restaurant in town, but after a few seconds of stunned silence, I backed down and suggested a good old Chinese meal. Thought we could share a buffet and all use chopsticks – it would be fun. My god, you'd think I'd suggested a strip club in Vegas!'

Doug laughed, the last of his whisky sloshing in the glass held close to his slightly rounded belly.

'But actually, it is quite ridiculous. It'll be exactly the same as ever. We'll go to the same place, meet at the same time, eat, drink and even leave at the same time. Sue will go on about calories and carbohydrates, Fran will take fifteen minutes to decide and then end up with the same pasta dish she always has. Mary, bless her, will do the same and then drink a few too many glasses of wine and end up getting tearful.'

Doug smiled and without comment got up to replenish his glass then sat down next to Winnifred on the sofa and placed his hand over hers in her lap.

'What's this all about? Really? Why is all this silliness suddenly bothering you? I mean, take poor Mary - how often does she get to go out? That bugger of a husband never takes her anywhere, he's too busy drinking the house dry. Can you honestly blame her for making the most of it when she gets a chance?'

'Oh god, yes, poor Mary; she looked awful last time. Not well at all.'

'Honestly Love, a night out with you lot once every six months is probably the extent of her social life. And you begrudge her always choosing her favourite meal of spaghetti carbonara?'

'How do you know she always has spaghetti carbonara?'

Doug shook his head, the sofa jiggling with his heavy laughter.

'I didn't know. It was just a lucky guess.'

Winnifred freed her hand from his and reached over for her glass of wine, giving him a sideways look, one of her mock-disapproving frowns, trying not to laugh herself.

'Ah, come on Winnie, you'll still have a good time. And that's what it's all about. Sometimes it's the routine and the sameness of things – familiarity I suppose that bring us comfort – security.'

'Hm, maybe. Don't mind me, I love them all really.' Winnie gazed into the wood-burning stove at the flames flickering inside. Doug usually had a good way of summing things up.

Since their two daughters had left home quite a few years ago now, their lives had fallen into a very solid routine which seldom varied. And although they enjoyed their comfortable life, in this instant, it irked her to realise that perhaps she wasn't so different from her friends after all.

'I was looking at online courses today, in my lunch hour.'

'Hm.' Doug had returned to his chair by the fire.

'Oenology – the study of wine. The advanced course. I'm going to register for it.'

'You've been saying that for ages.'

'Yes, I know. But finally, I'm really going to do it.'

'Good. About time. Go for it.'

It was a little white lie; Winnie hadn't been looking at online courses in her lunch hour at all. She intended to, almost every day, but once inside the work canteen she usually got chatting with someone over a quick bite to eat and the time just disappeared.

But by saying it out loud to Doug, it felt just that little bit closer to reality. And predictably, she felt guilty for lying to him, knowing it would spur her on to make it the truth – tomorrow. Having already completed the basic oenology course a couple of years ago, she would enrol for the advanced course tomorrow for definite.

And maybe in a few weeks' time when she met up with her friends again, she'd be able to offer expert advice on their choice of wine – even if it was at the same old Italian restaurant.

Printed in Great Britain
by Amazon